# this book is dedicated to harper

a giant amongst tiny monsters.

legal

# GRONK

volume four

## a monster's story

### a comic by katie cook

you can find gronk online here: www.gronkcomic.com
you can find katie online here: www.katiecandraw.com

colors for the interior pages by kate carleton and katie herself
the colors for the FCBD story by heather breckel

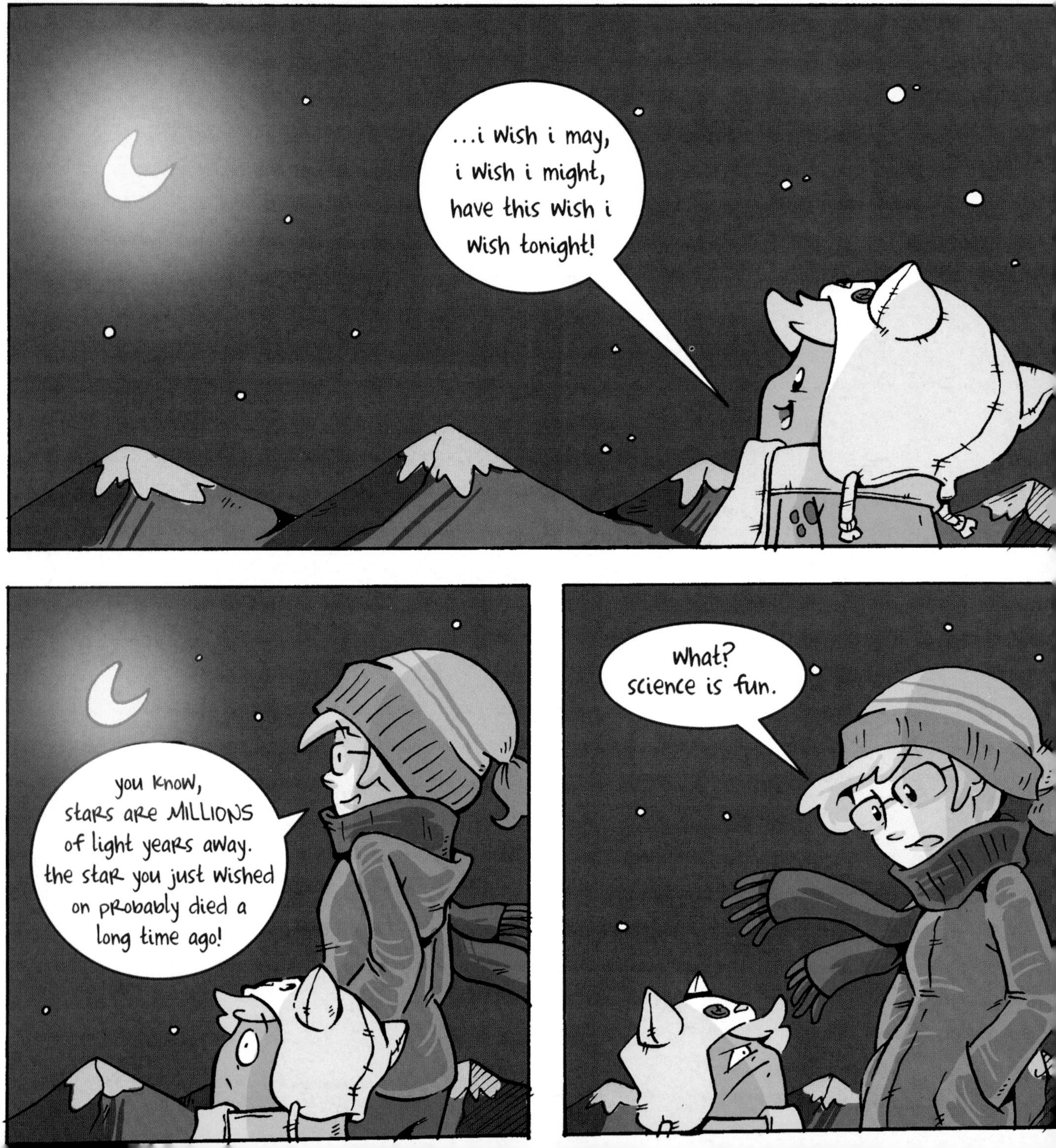
...i wish i may, i wish i might, have this wish i wish tonight!
you know, stars are MILLIONS of light years away. the star you just wished on probably died a long time ago!
what? science is fun.

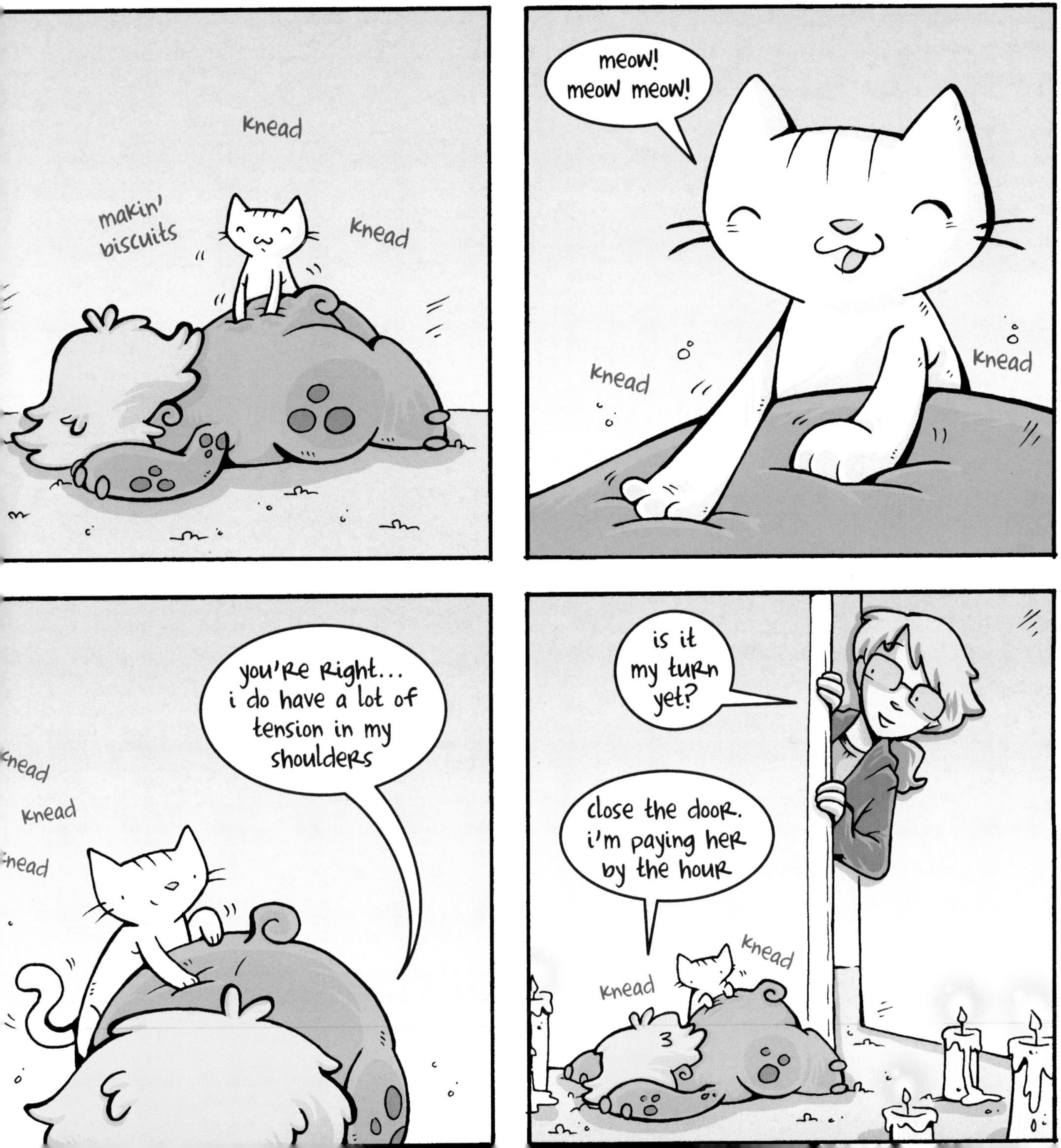
knead
makin' biscuits
knead
meow! meow meow!
knead
knead
you're right... i do have a lot of tension in my shoulders
nead
knead
nead
is it my turn yet?
close the door. i'm paying her by the hour
knead
knead

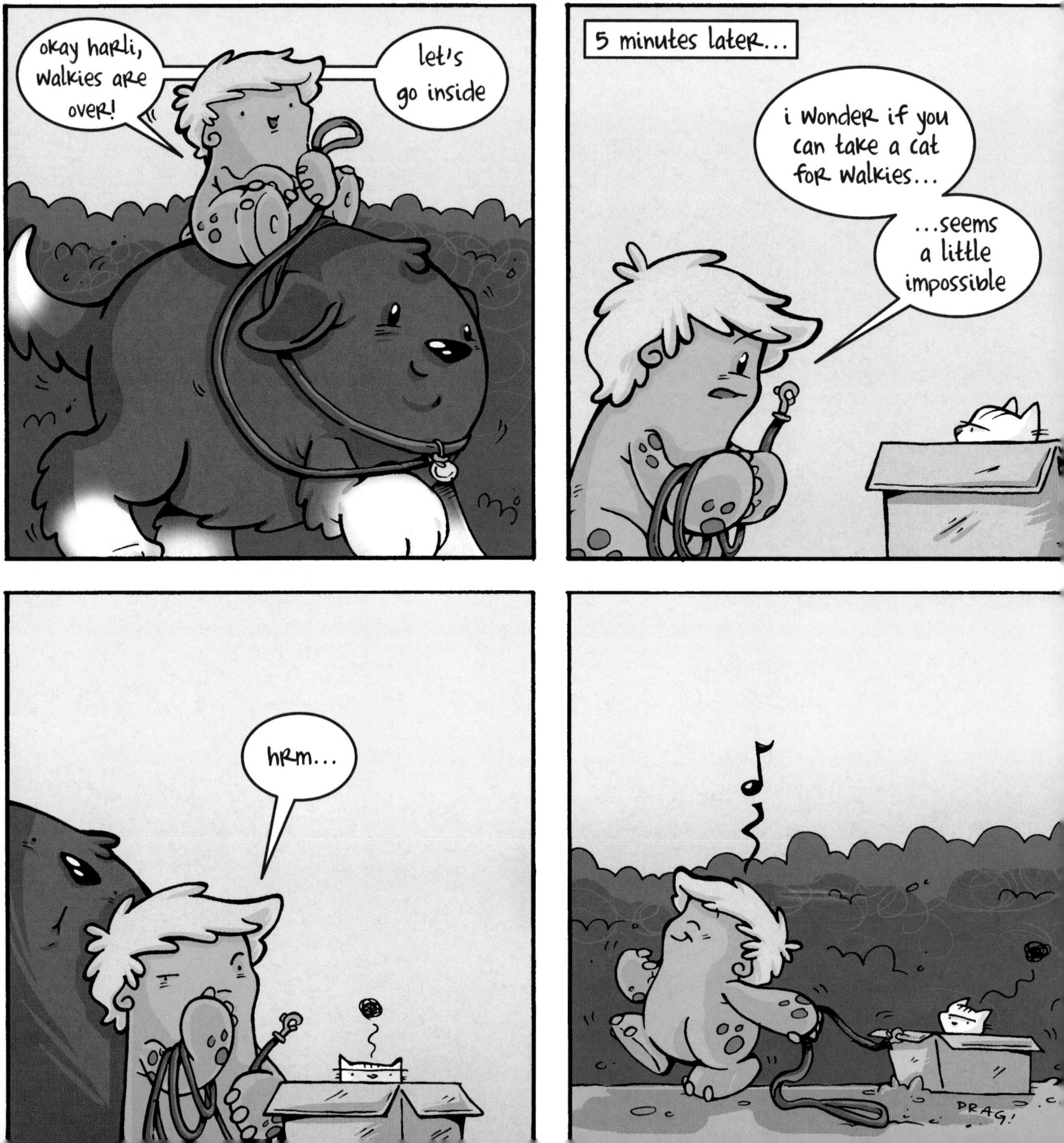
okay harli, walkies are over!
let's go inside
5 minutes later...
i wonder if you can take a cat for walkies...
...seems a little impossible
hrm...
DRAG!

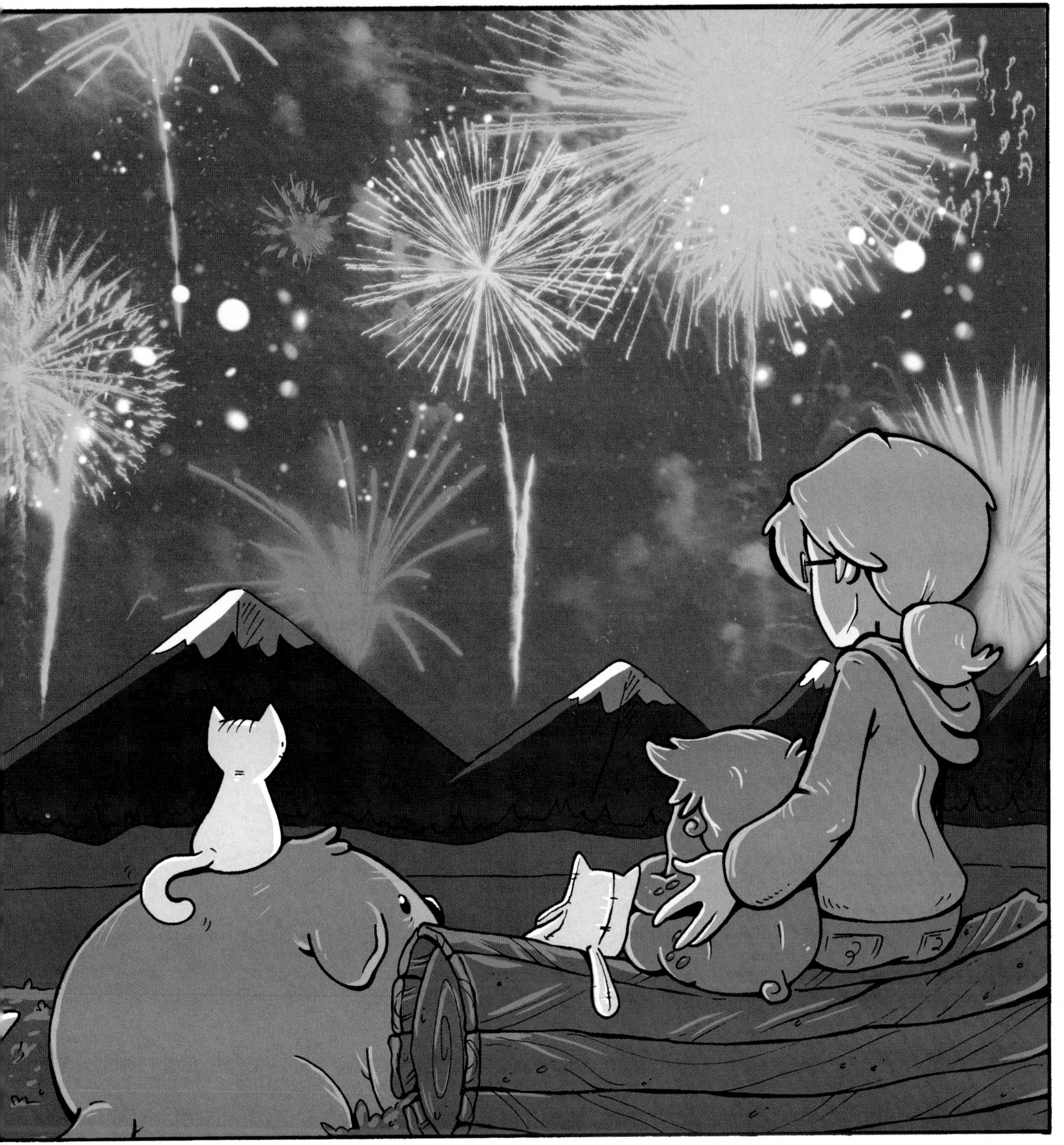

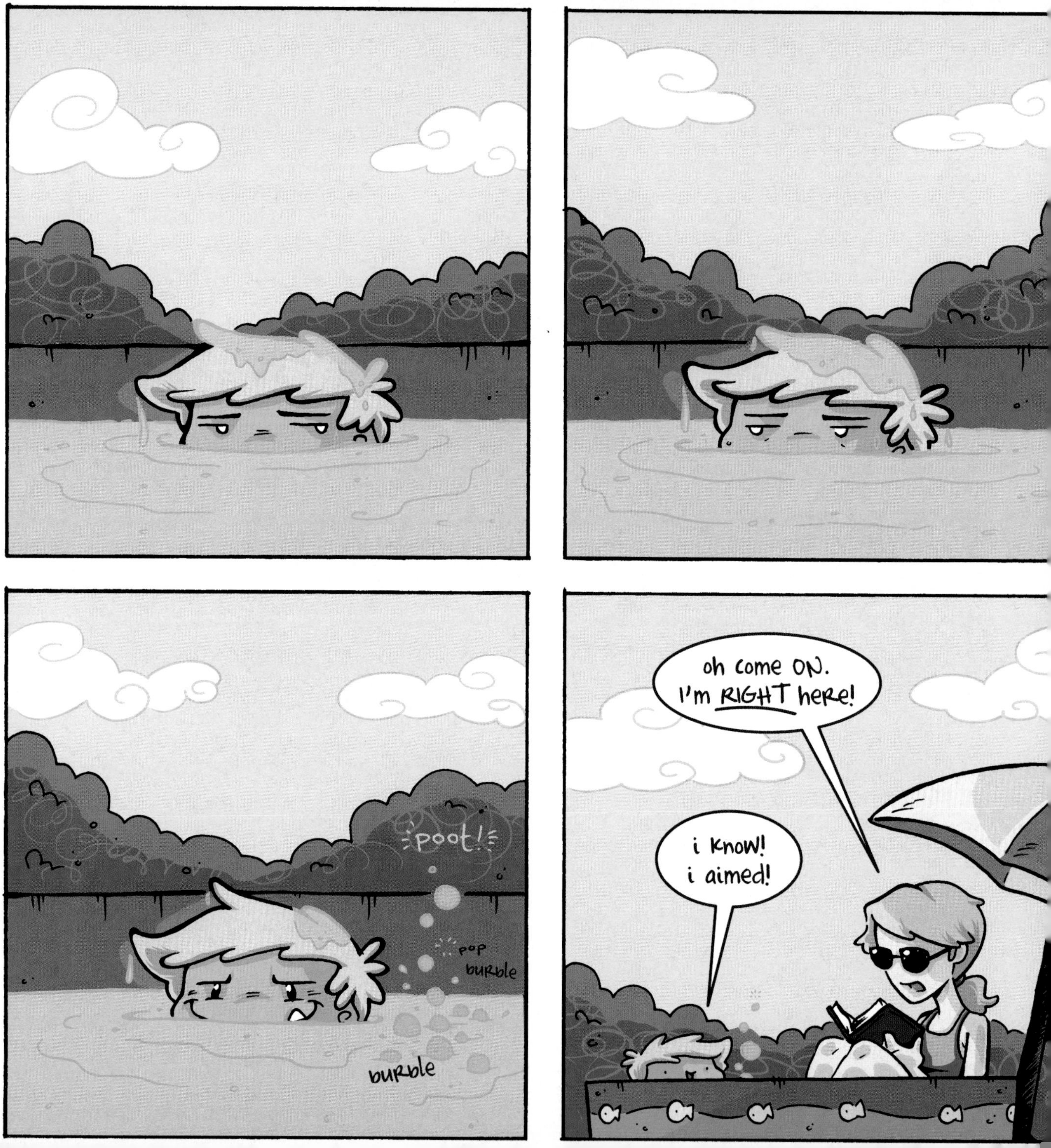
poot!
pop
burble
burble
oh come ON.
I'm RIGHT here!
i know!
i aimed!

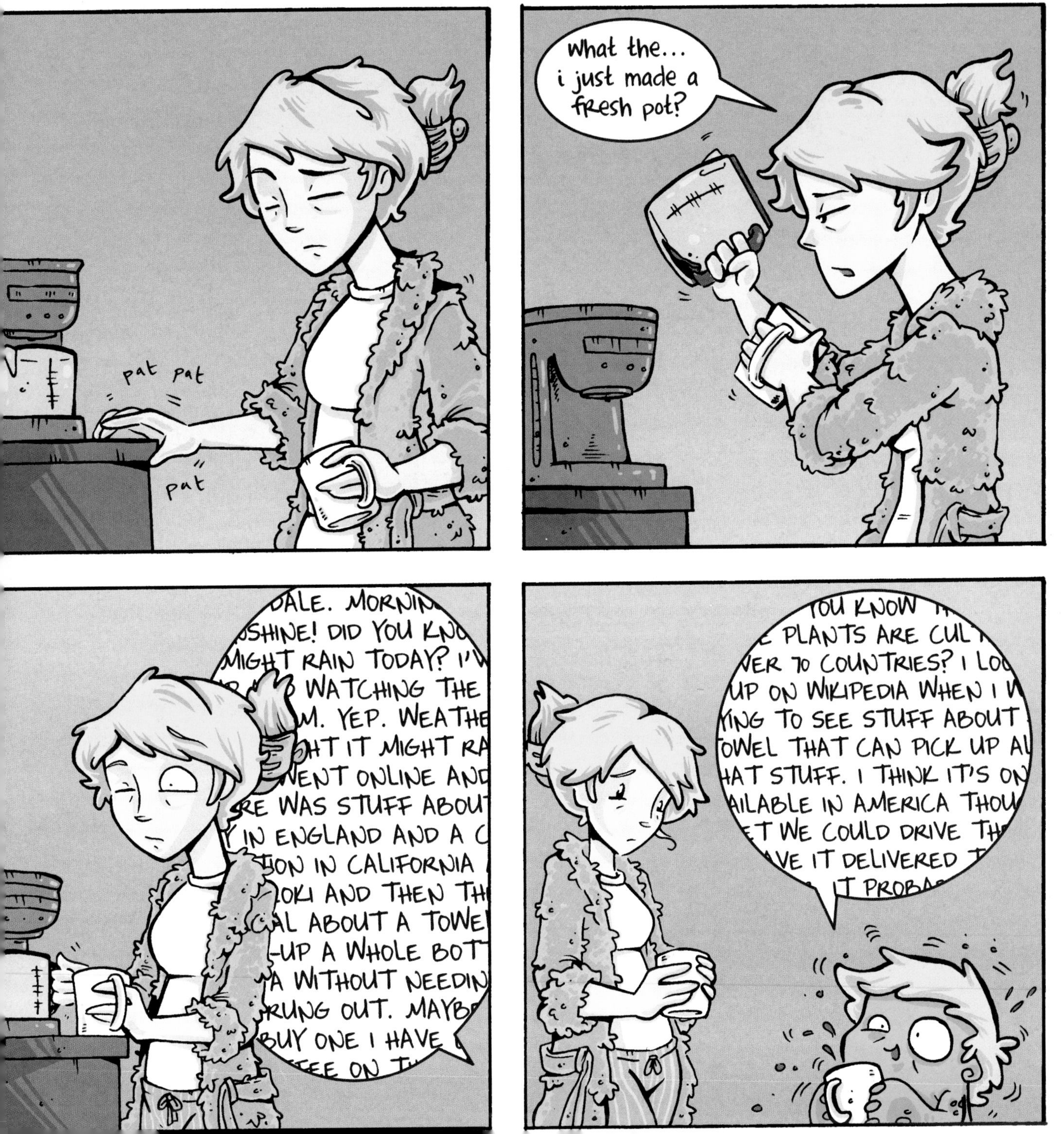

pat pat
pat
What the... i just made a fresh pot?
DALE. MORNIN
SHINE! DID YOU KN
MIGHT RAIN TODAY? I'
WATCHING THE
M. YEP. WEATHE
HT IT MIGHT RA
WENT ONLINE AND
RE WAS STUFF ABOUT
IN ENGLAND AND A C
TION IN CALIFORNIA
LOKI AND THEN TH
AL ABOUT A TOWE
-UP A WHOLE BOT
A WITHOUT NEEDIN
RUNG OUT. MAYB
BUY ONE I HAVE
YOU KNOW
PLANTS ARE CUL
VER 70 COUNTRIES? I LO
UP ON WIKIPEDIA WHEN I W
YING TO SEE STUFF ABOUT
TOWEL THAT CAN PICK UP A
HAT STUFF. I THINK IT'S ON
AILABLE IN AMERICA THOU
T WE COULD DRIVE TH
AVE IT DELIVERED T
T PROBA

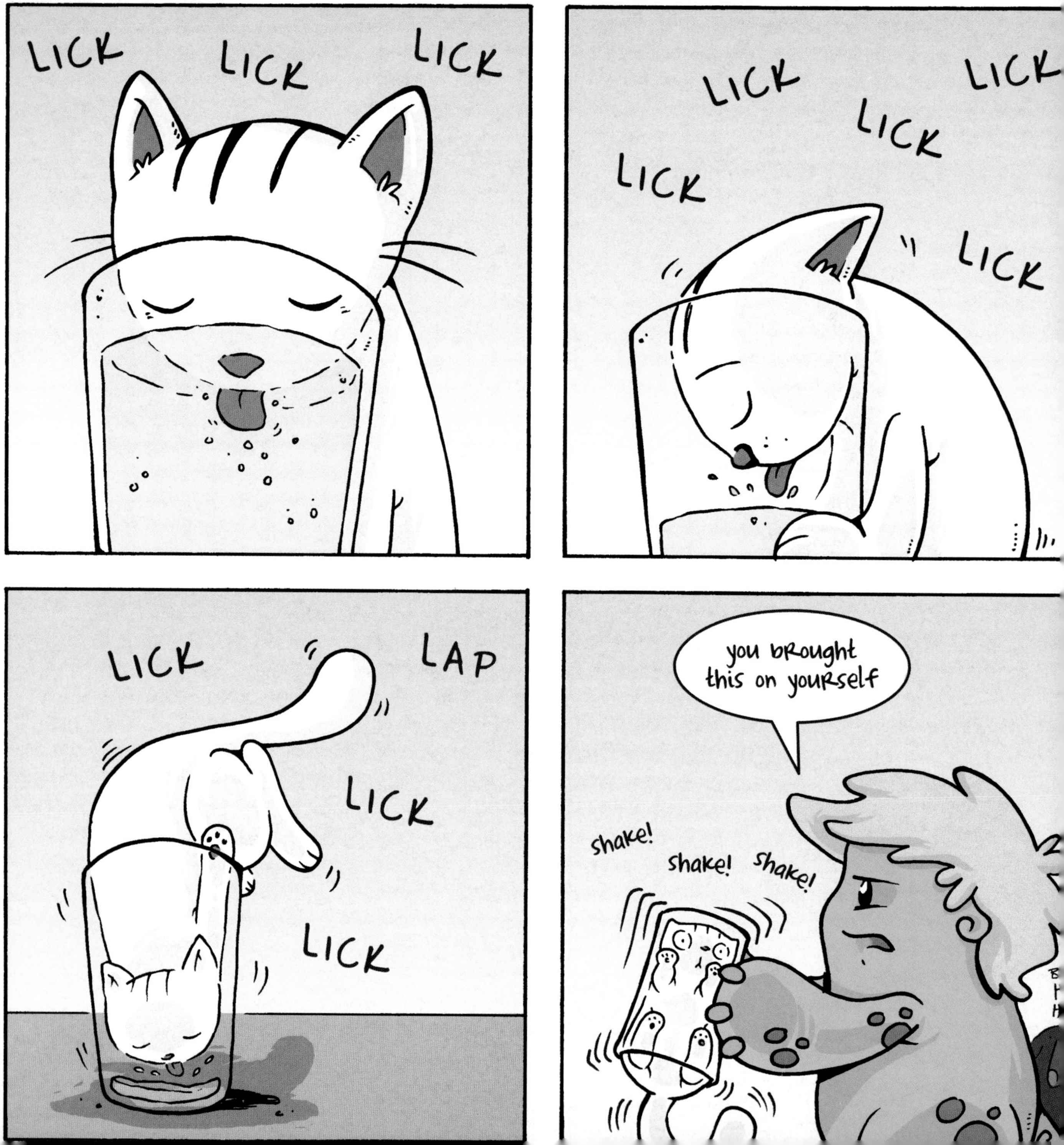
LICK
LICK
LICK
LICK
LICK
LICK
LICK
LICK
LAP
LICK
LICK
you brought this on yourself
shake!
shake!
shake!

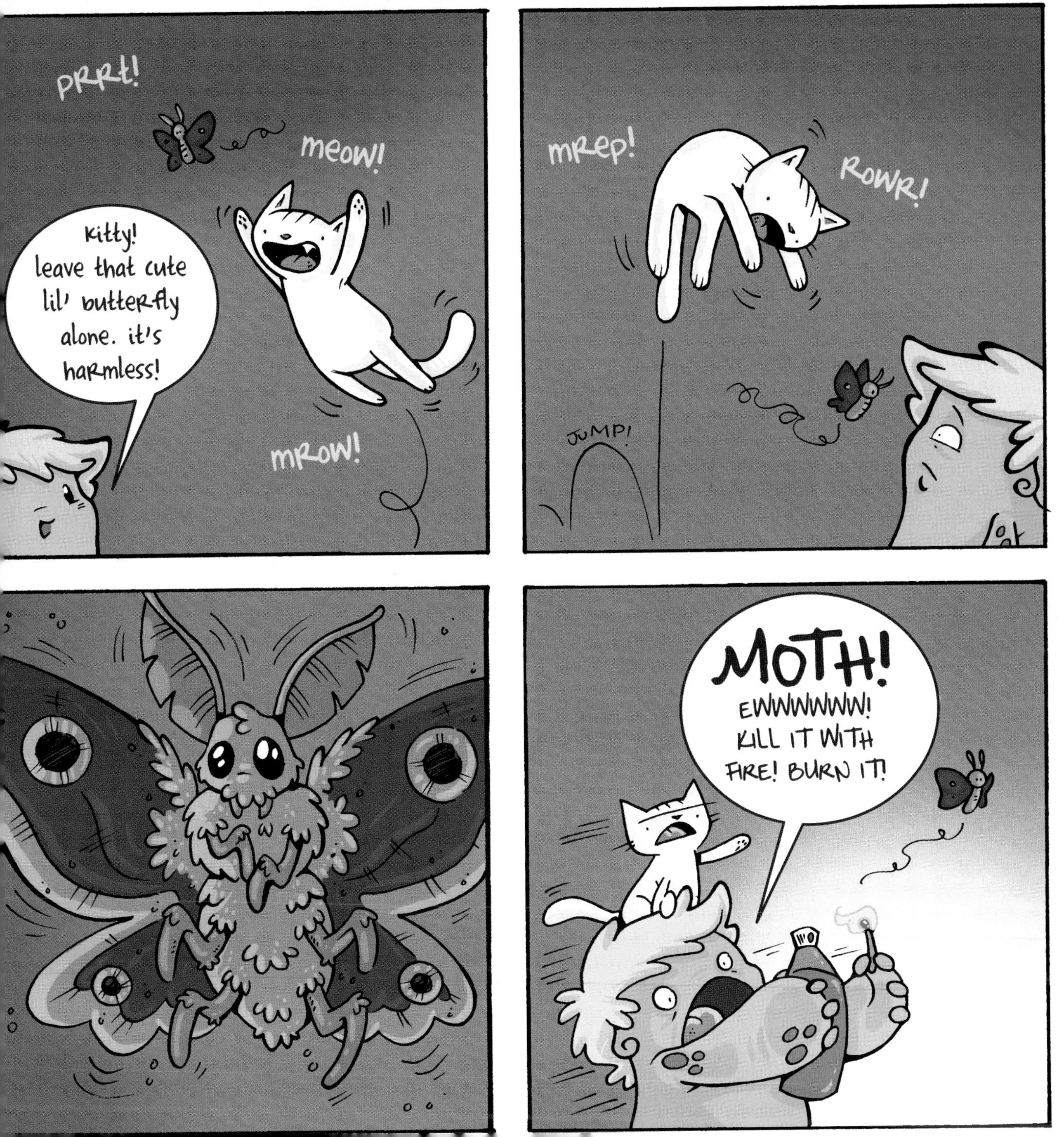
PRRt!
meow!
Kitty! leave that cute lil' butterfly alone. it's harmless!
MROW!
mREp!
ROWR!
JUMP!
MOTH!
EWWWWWW! KILL IT WITH FIRE! BURN IT!

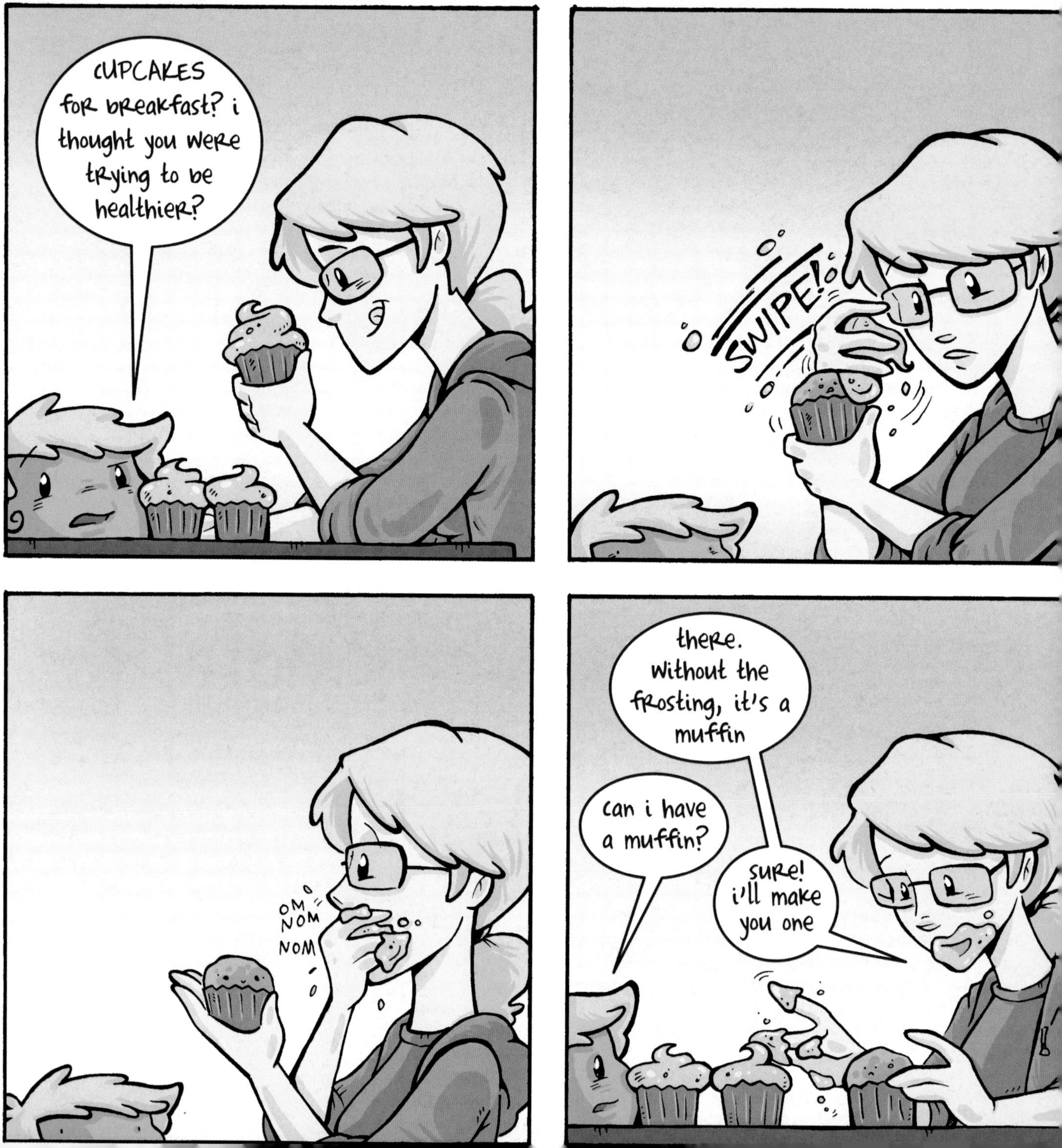
CUPCAKES for breakfast? i thought you were trying to be healthier?
SWIPE!
OM NOM NOM
there. without the frosting, it's a muffin
can i have a muffin?
sure! i'll make you one

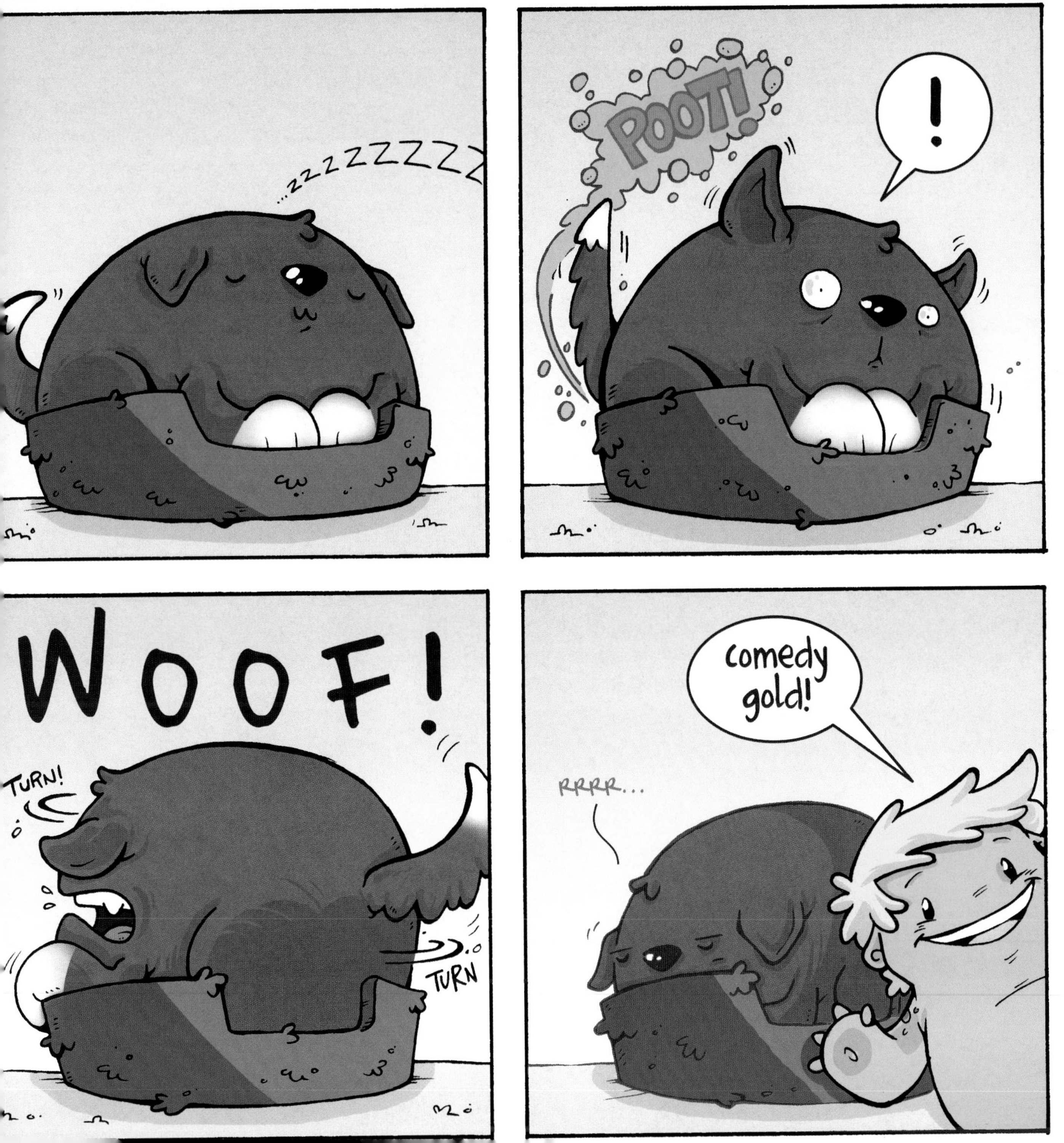

...zzZZZZZZZ
POOT!
!
WOOF!
TURN!
TURN
comedy gold!
RRRR...

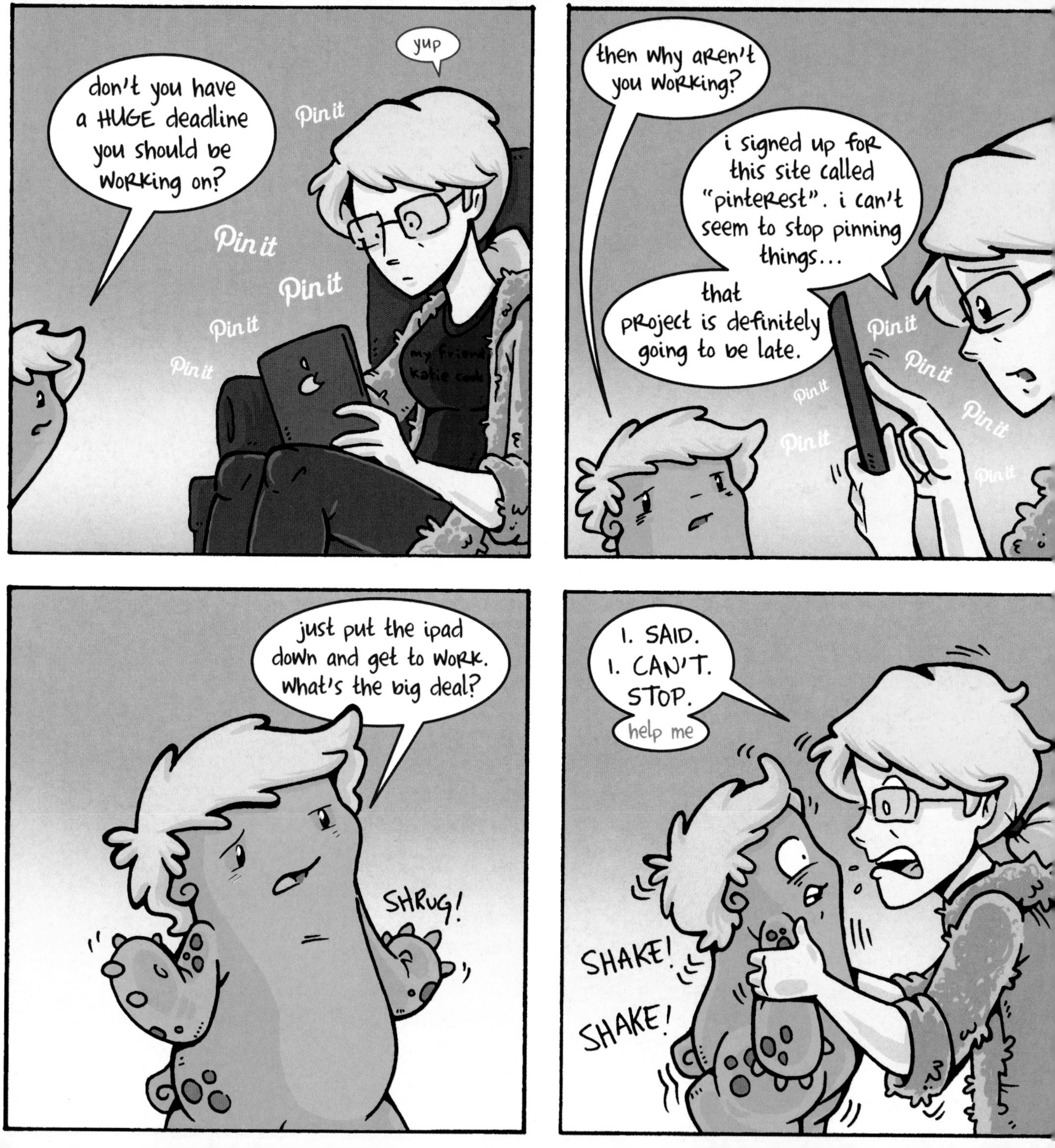
yup
don't you have a HUGE deadline you should be working on?
Pin it
Pin it
Pin it
Pin it
Pin it
my friend katie cook
then why aren't you working?
i signed up for this site called "pinterest". i can't seem to stop pinning things...
that project is definitely going to be late.
Pin it
Pin it
Pin it
Pin it
Pin it
Pin it
just put the ipad down and get to work. what's the big deal?
SHRUG!
I. SAID. I. CAN'T. STOP.
help me
SHAKE!
SHAKE!

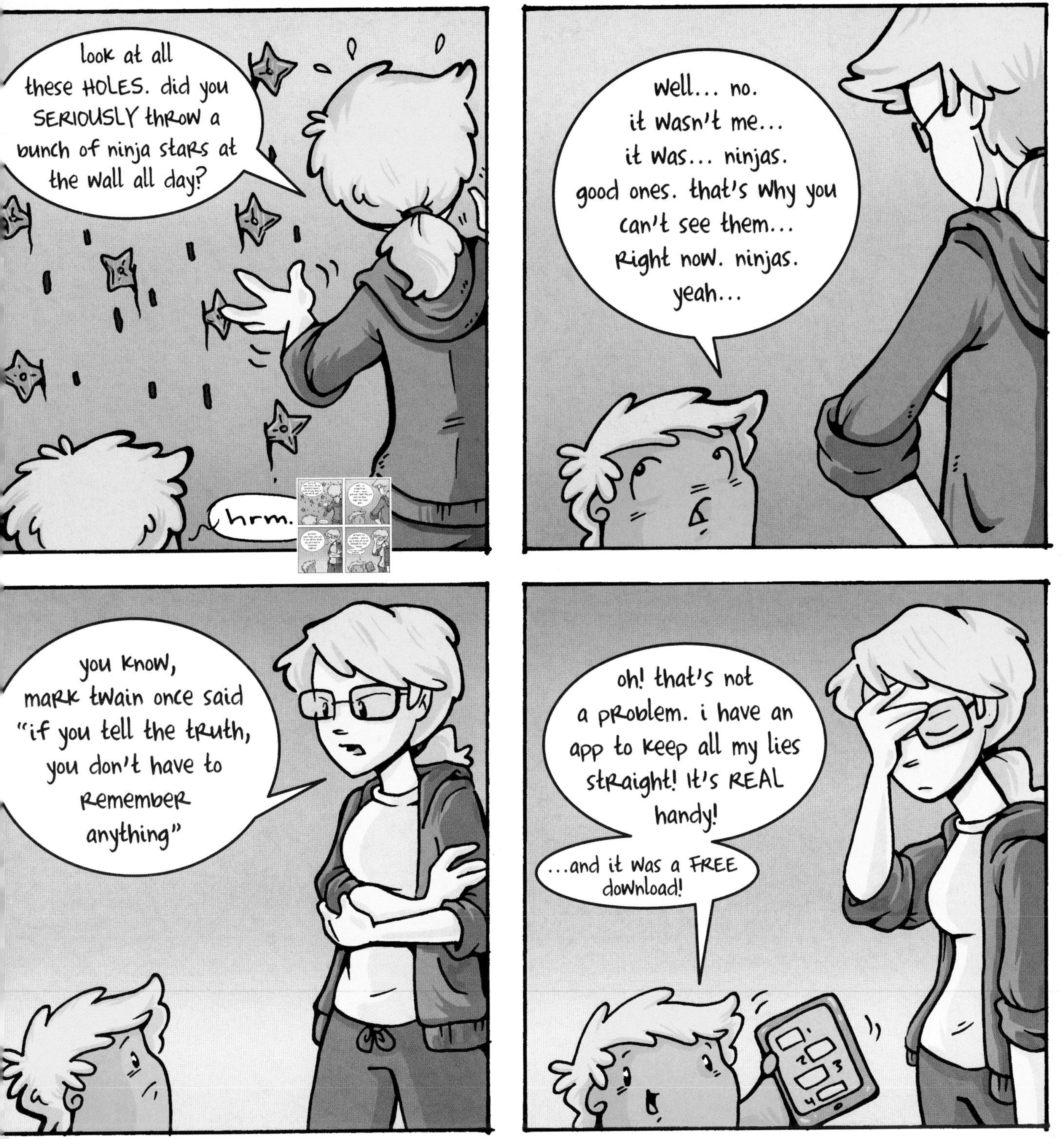
look at all these HOLES. did you SERIOUSLY throw a bunch of ninja stars at the wall all day?
hrm.
well... no. it wasn't me... it was... ninjas. good ones. that's why you can't see them... right now. ninjas. yeah...
you know, mark twain once said "if you tell the truth, you don't have to remember anything"
oh! that's not a problem. i have an app to keep all my lies straight! It's REAL handy!
...and it was a FREE download!

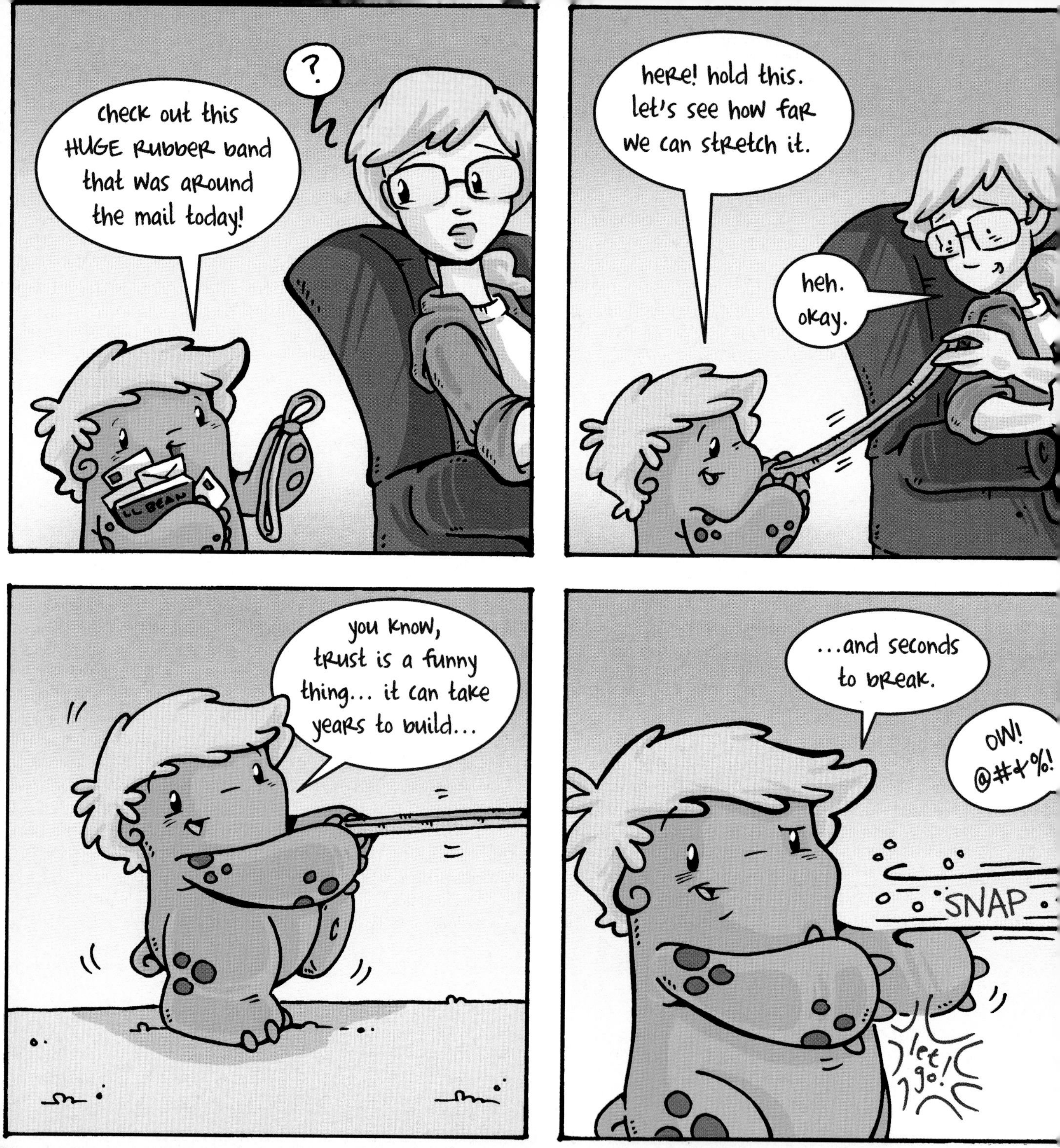
check out this HUGE rubber band that was around the mail today!
?
LL BEAN
here! hold this. let's see how far we can stretch it.
heh. okay.
you know, trust is a funny thing... it can take years to build...
...and seconds to break.
OW! @#¢%!
SNAP
let go!

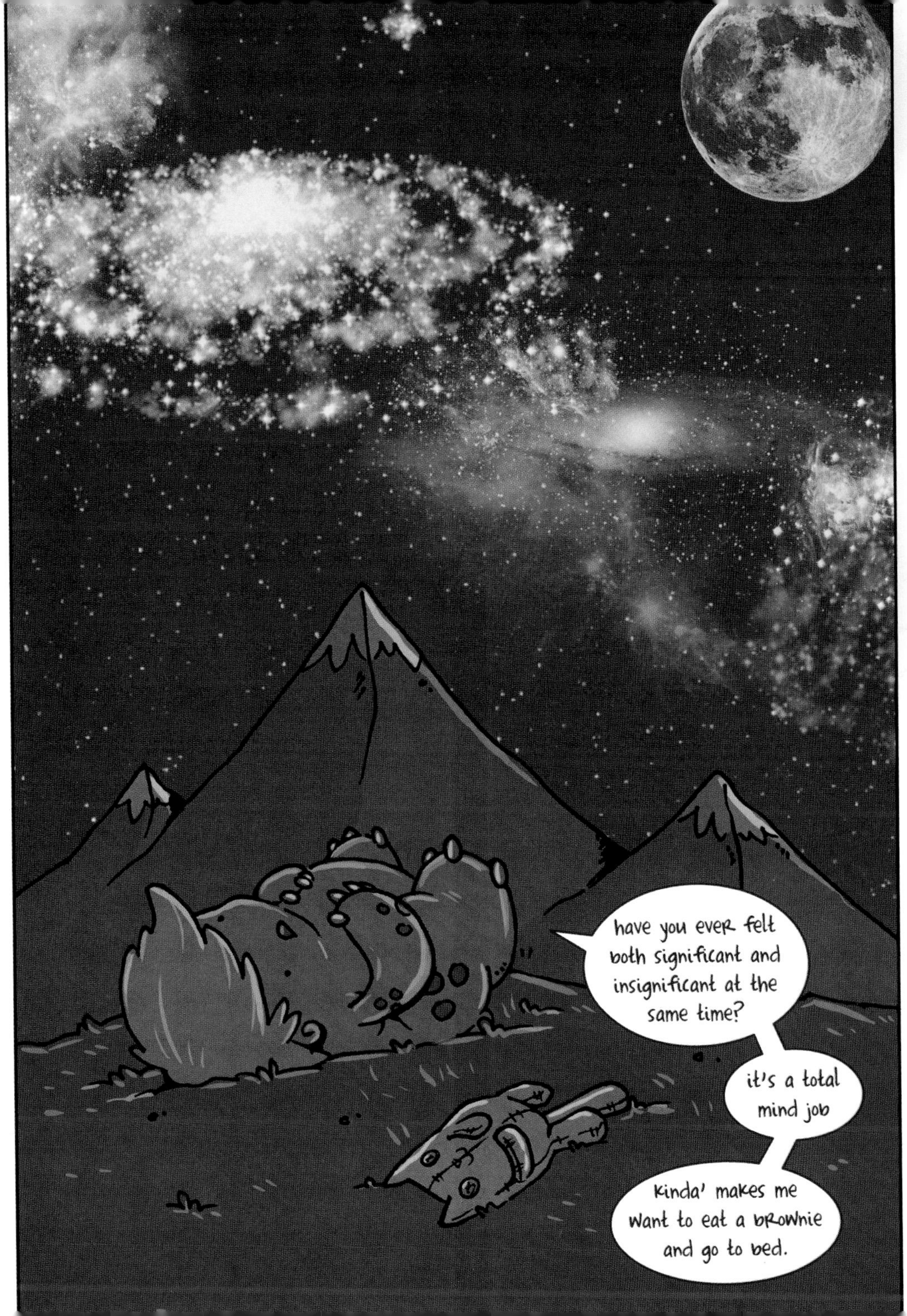

have you ever felt both significant and insignificant at the same time?
it's a total mind job
Kinda' makes me want to eat a brownie and go to bed.

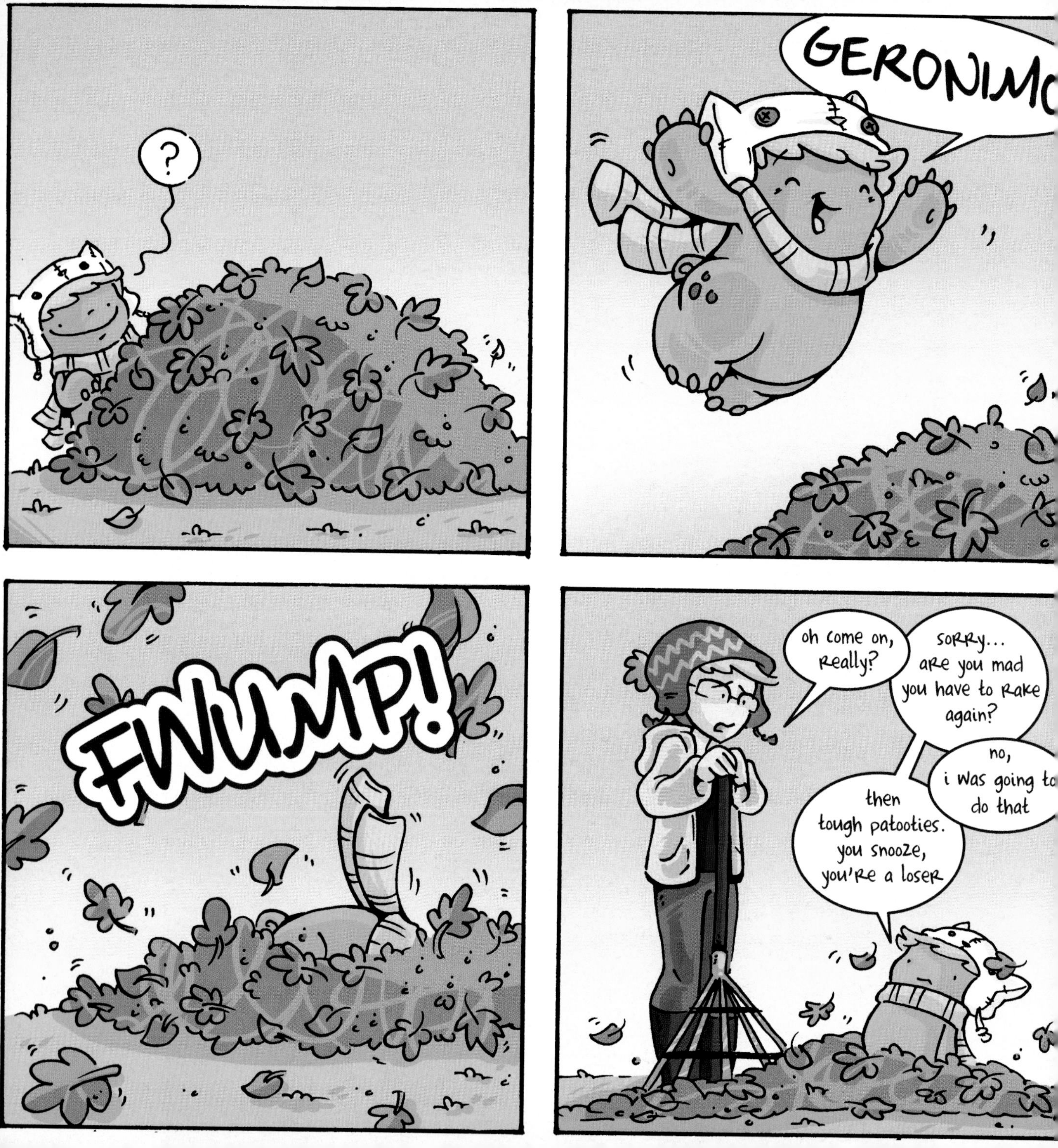
?
GERONIMO
FWUMP!
oh come on, Really?
SORRY... aRe you mad you have to Rake again?
no, i was going to do that
then tough patooties. you snooze, you're a loser

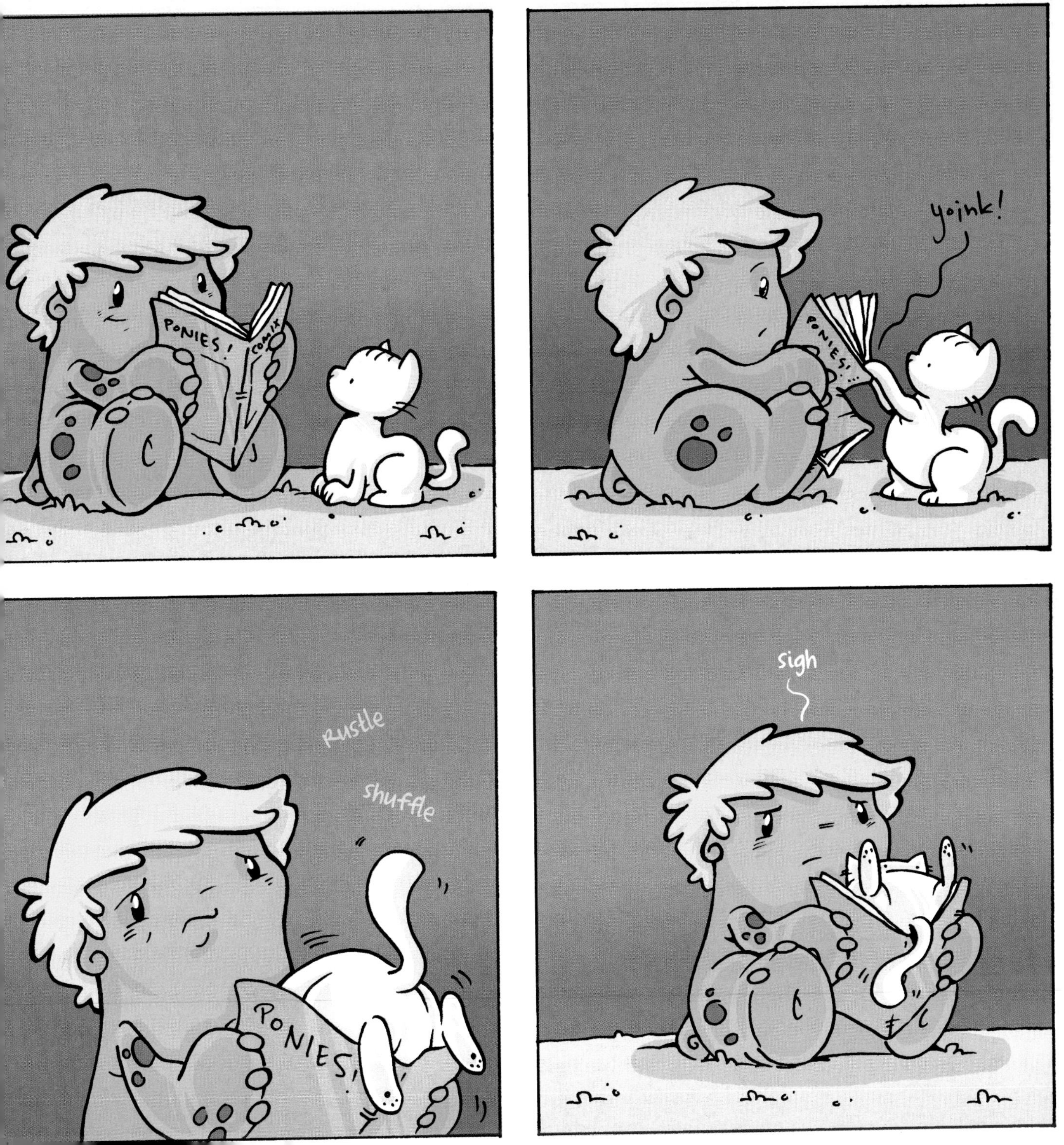
PONIES! COMIX
PONIES!...
yoink!
rustle
shuffle
PONIES!
sigh

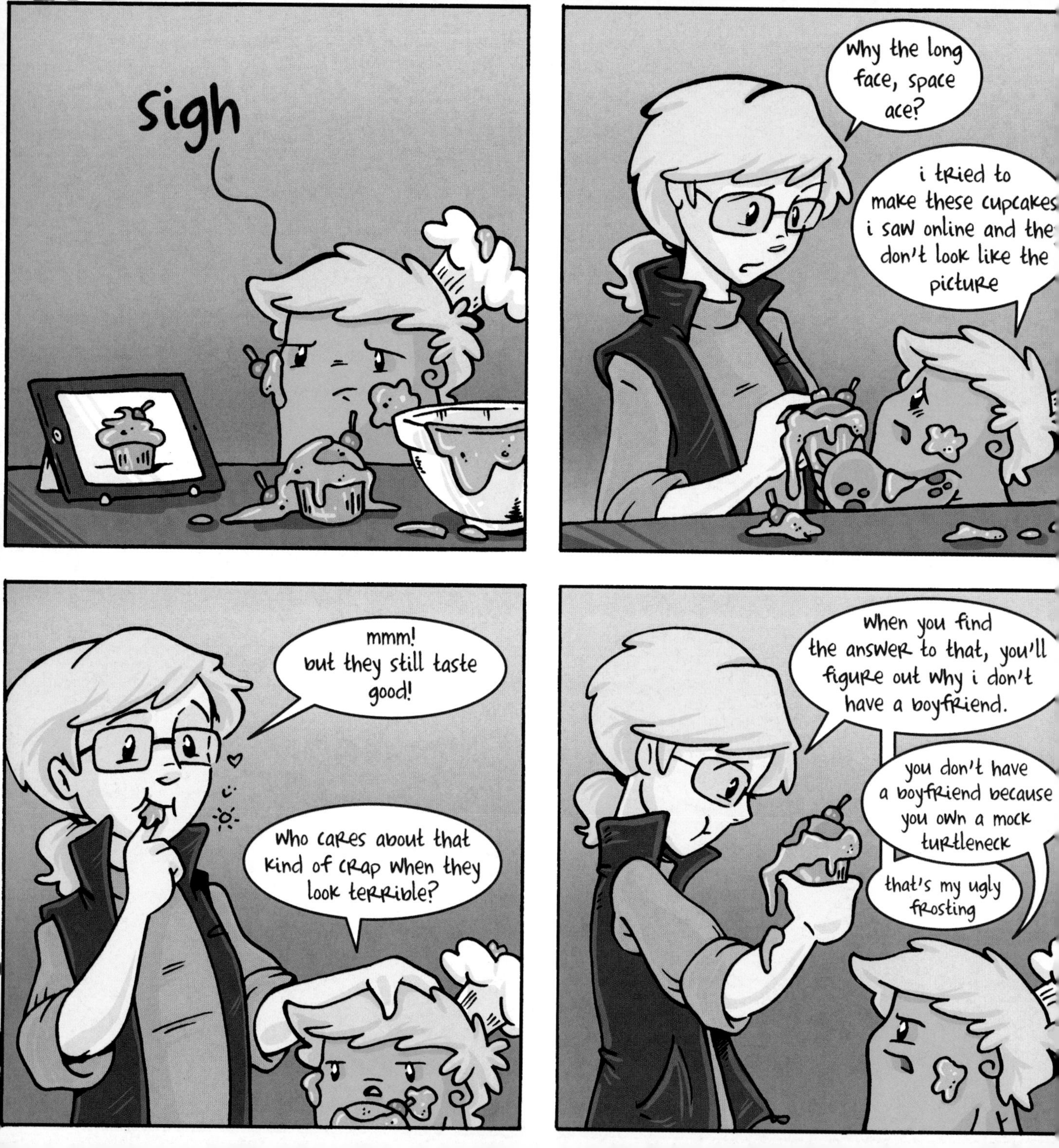
sigh
Why the long face, space ace?
i tried to make these cupcakes i saw online and the don't look like the picture
mmm! but they still taste good!
Who cares about that kind of crap when they look terrible?
When you find the answer to that, you'll figure out why i don't have a boyfriend.
you don't have a boyfriend because you own a mock turtleneck
that's my ugly frosting

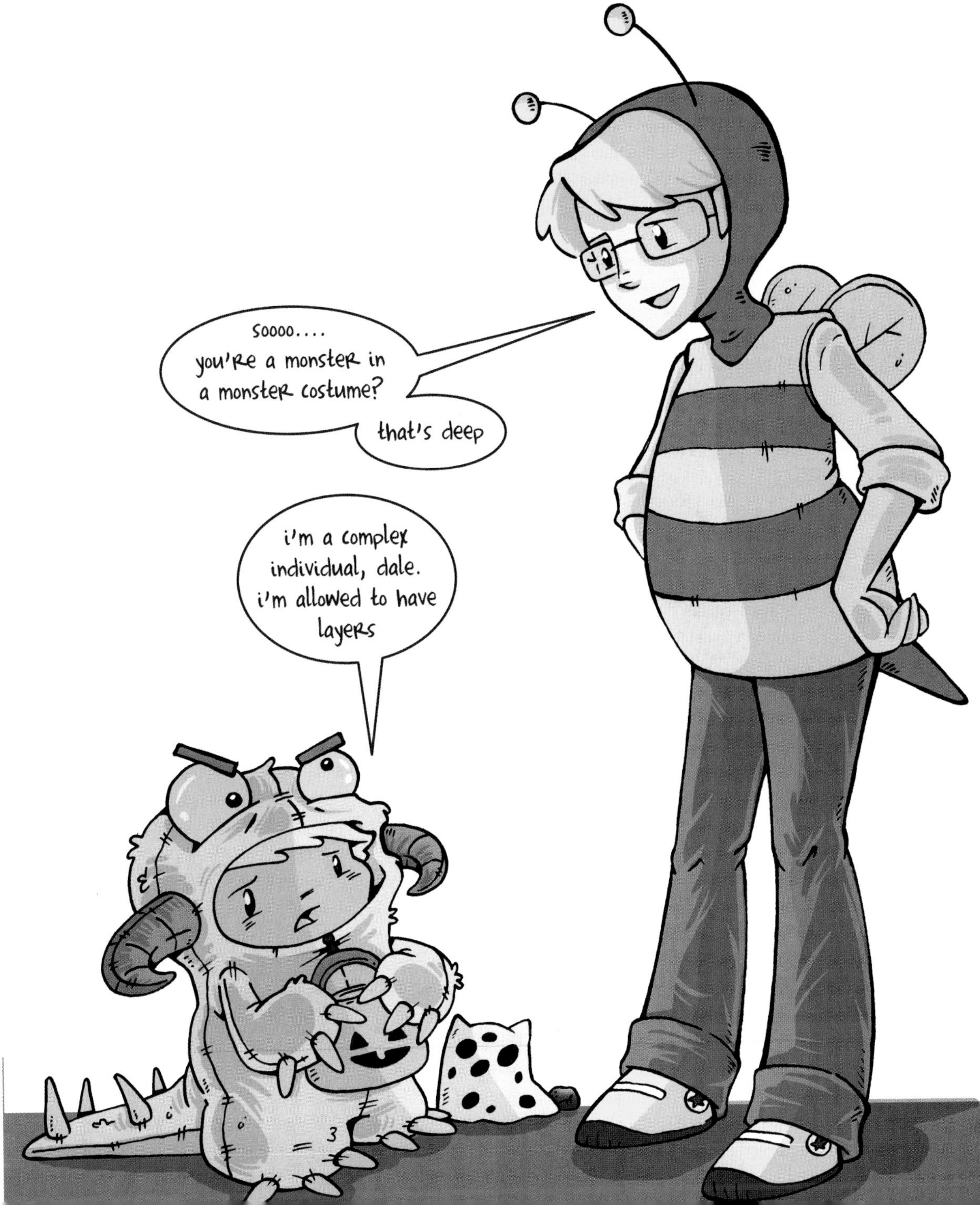
soooo....
you're a monster in
a monster costume?
that's deep
i'm a complex
individual, dale.
i'm allowed to have
layers

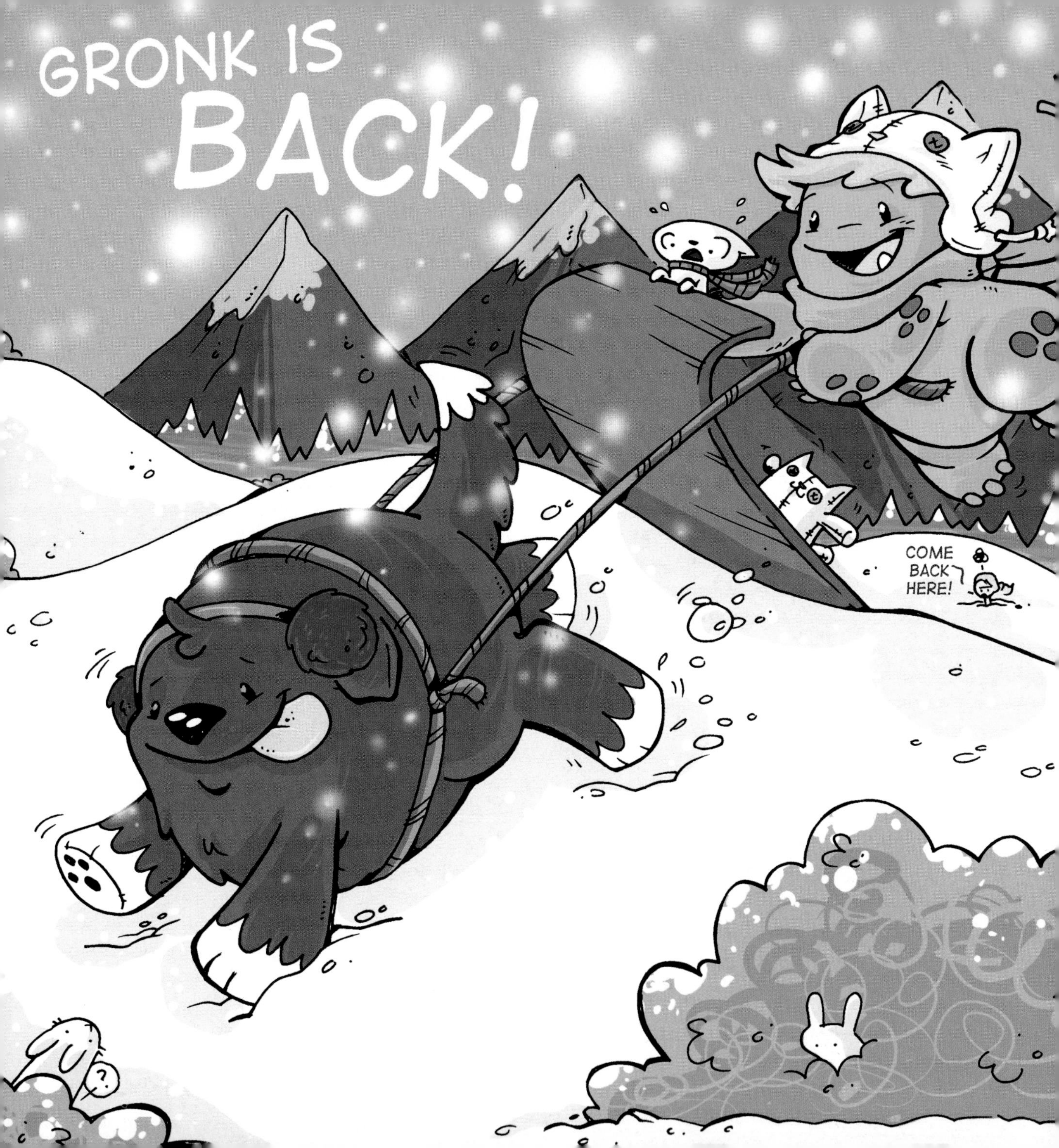
GRONK IS BACK!
COME BACK HERE!

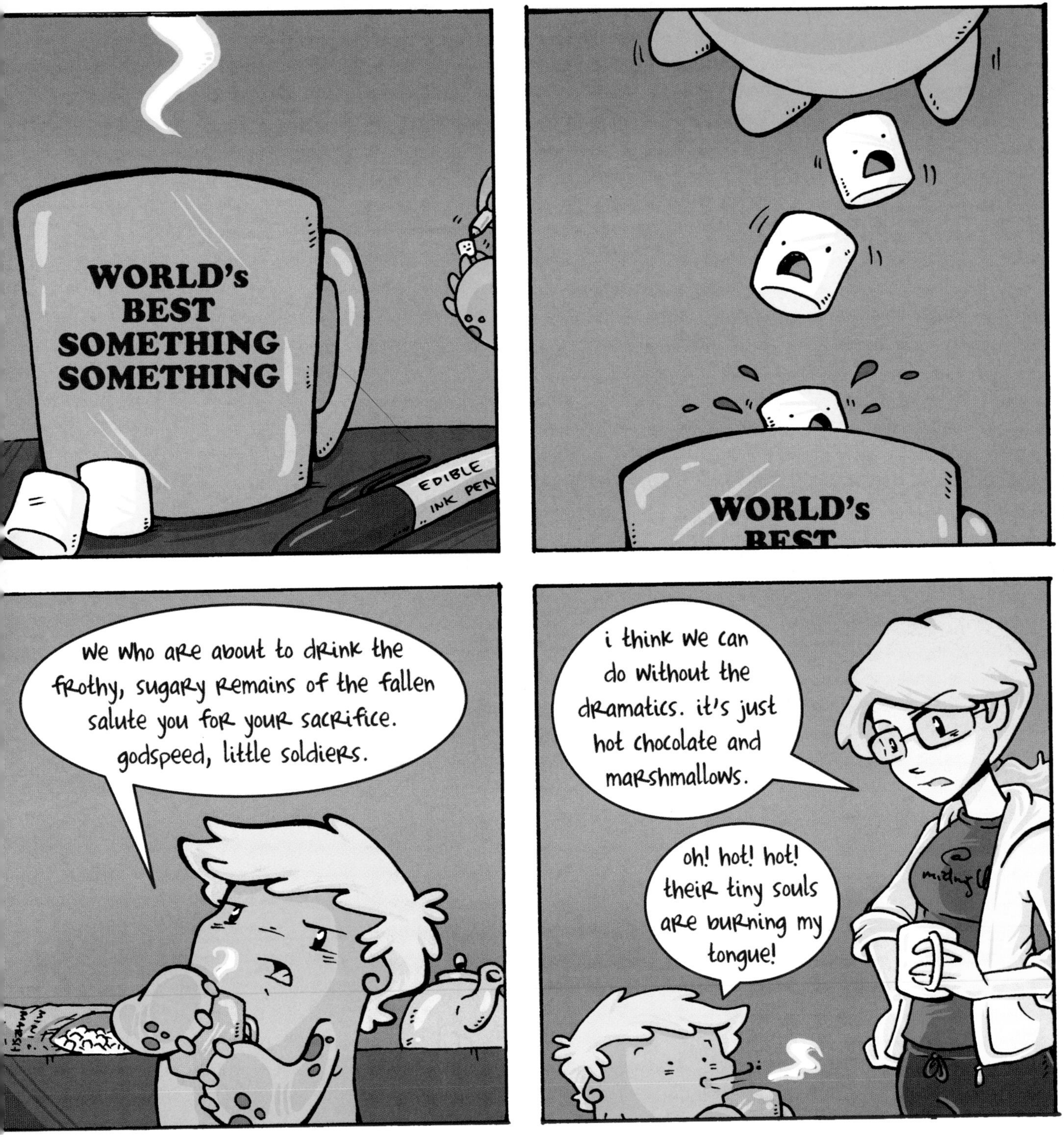

WORLD's BEST SOMETHING SOMETHING
EDIBLE INK PEN
WORLD's BEST
We who are about to drink the frothy, sugary remains of the fallen salute you for your sacrifice. godspeed, little soldiers.
i think we can do without the dramatics. it's just hot chocolate and marshmallows.
oh! hot! hot! their tiny souls are burning my tongue!

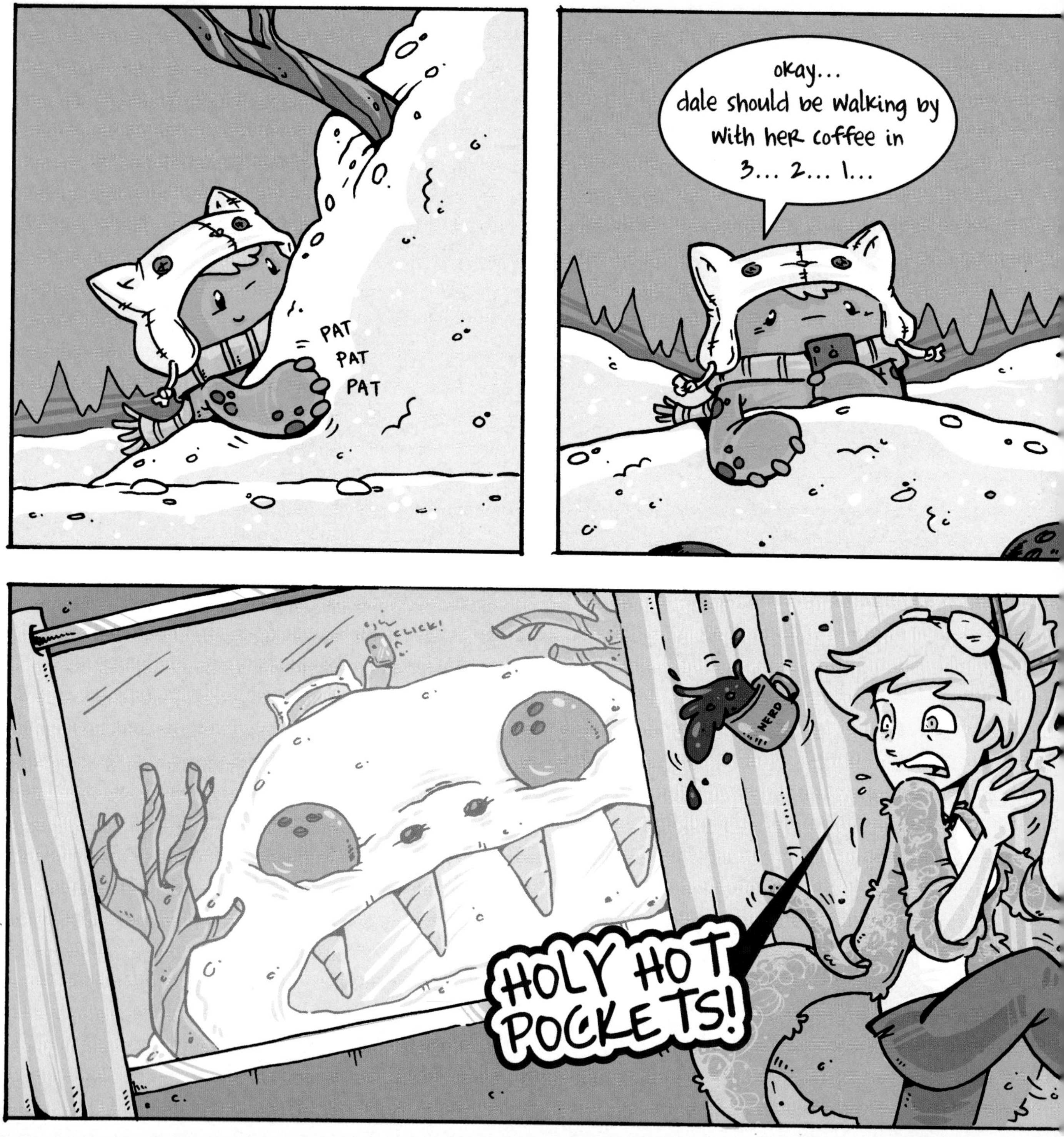
PAT
PAT
PAT
okay...
dale should be walking by
with her coffee in
3... 2... 1...
CLICK!
NERD
HOLY HOT
POCKETS!

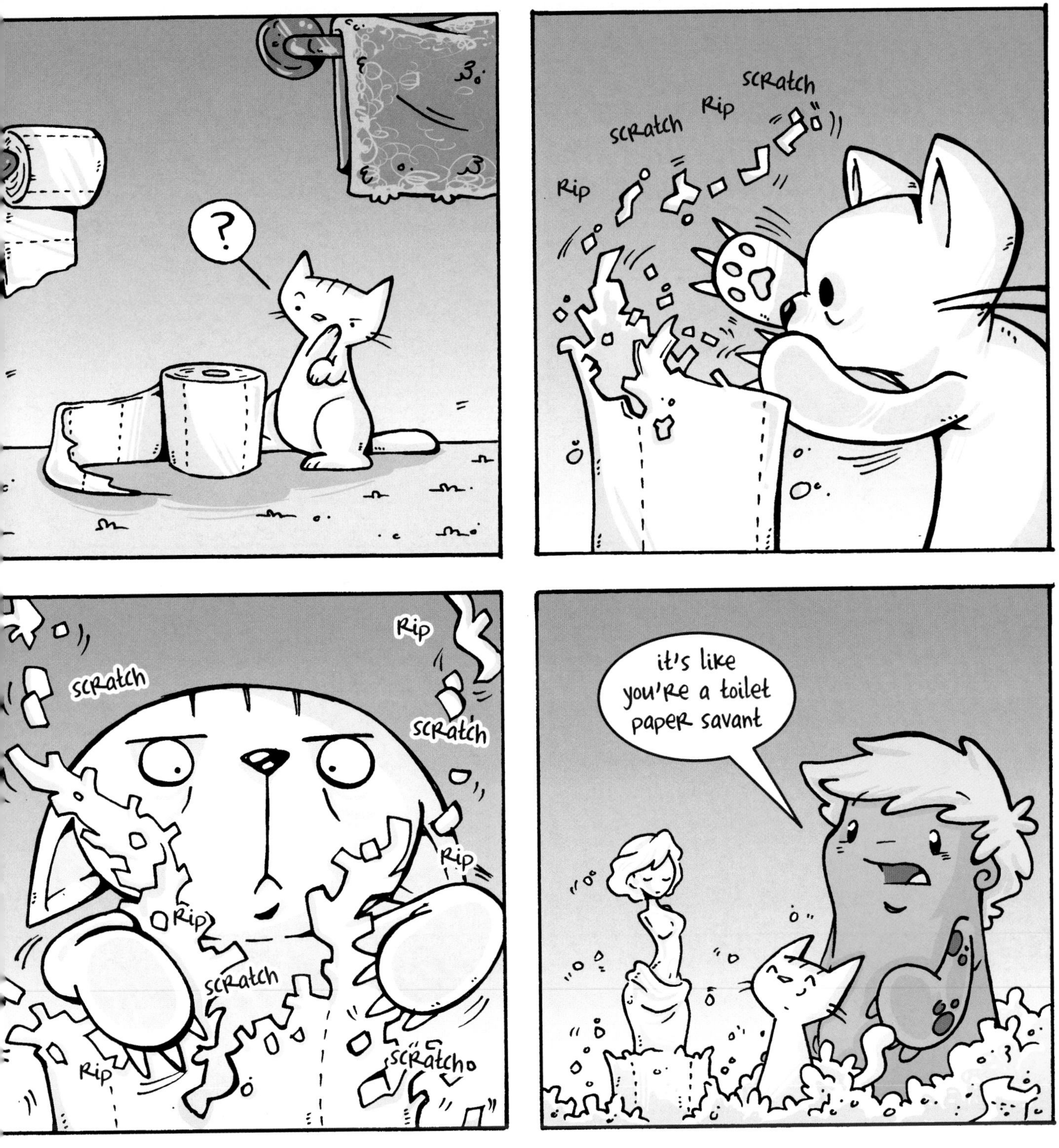
?
Rip
scratch
Rip
scratch
scratch
Rip
scratch
Rip
Rip
scratch
Rip
scratch
it's like you're a toilet paper savant

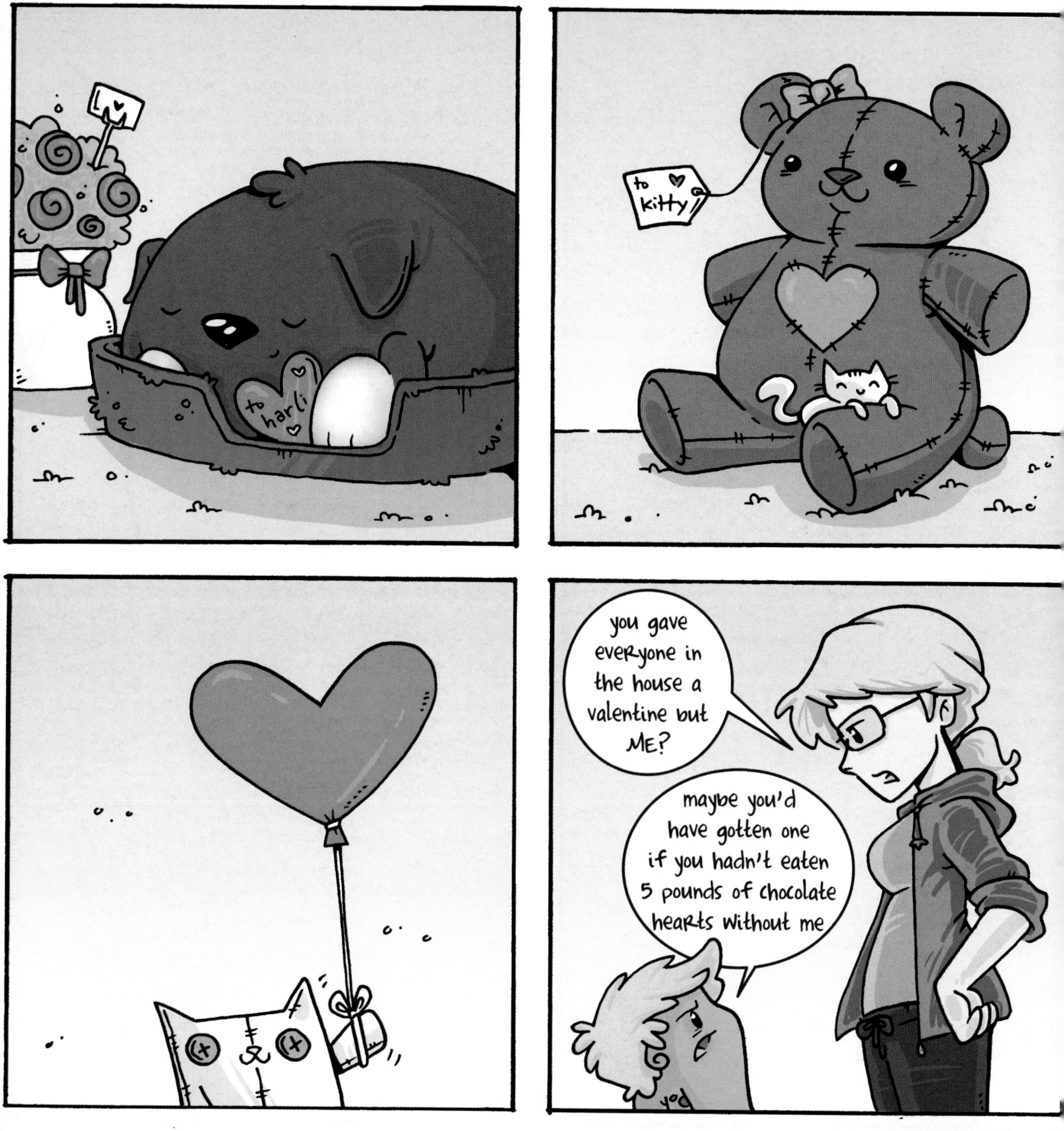
to harli
to kitty
you gave everyone in the house a valentine but ME?
maybe you'd have gotten one if you hadn't eaten 5 pounds of chocolate hearts without me

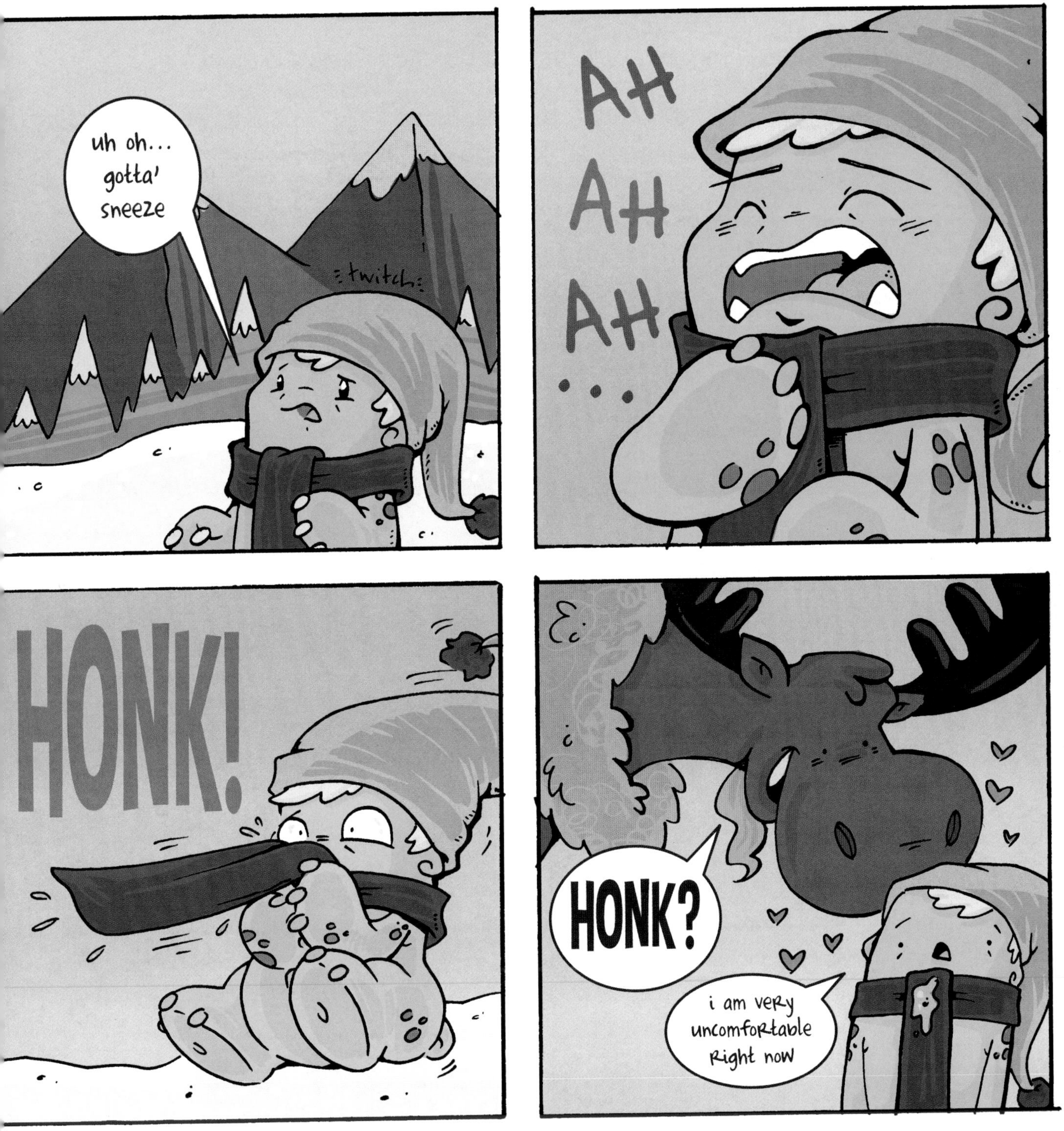
uh oh... gotta' sneeze
twitch
AH AH AH
HONK!
HONK?
i am very uncomfortable right now

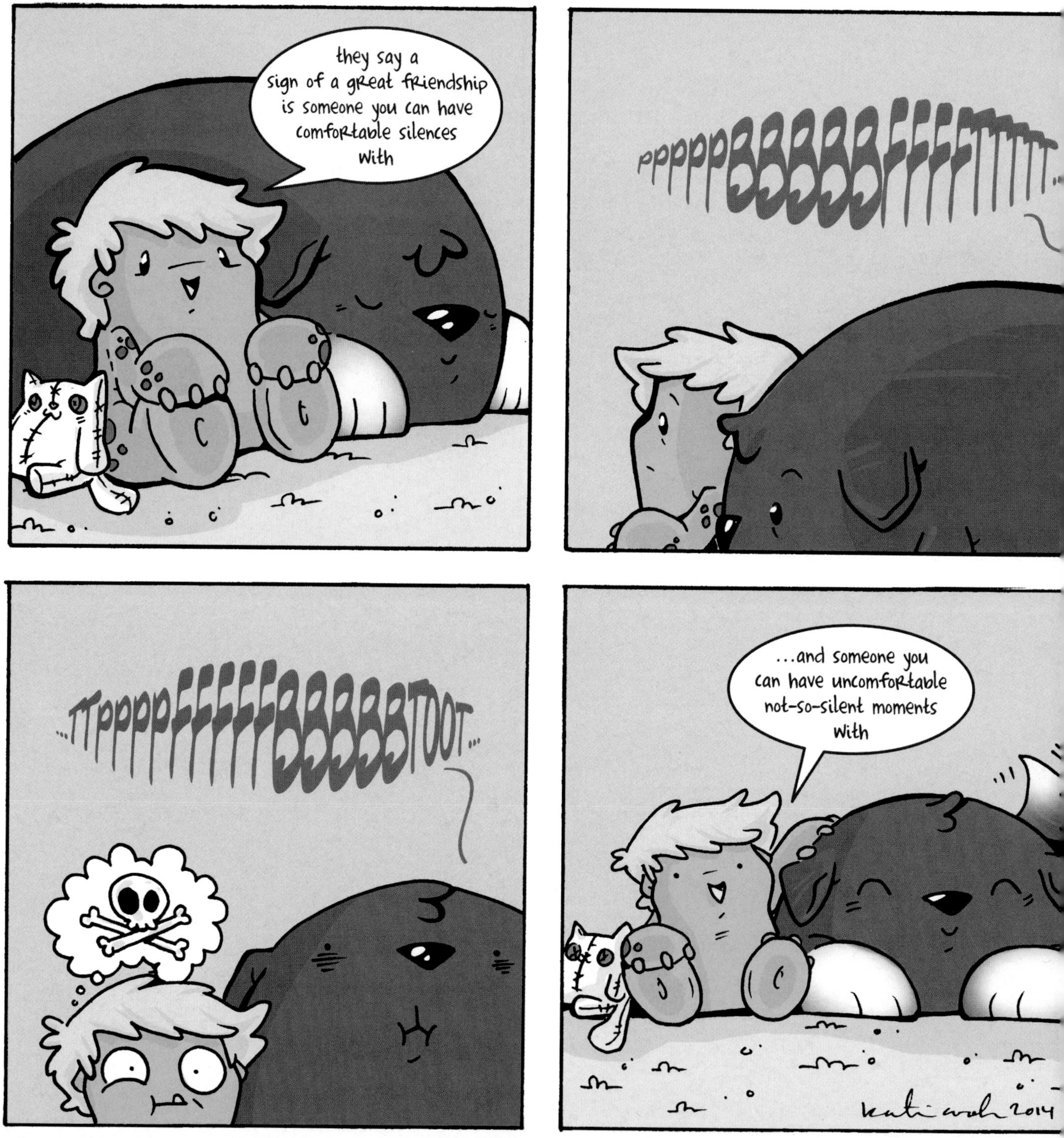
they say a sign of a great friendship is someone you can have comfortable silences with
PPPPPBBBBBBFFFFTTTTTT...
...TTPPPPFFFFFBBBBBTOOT...
...and someone you can have uncomfortable not-so-silent moments with
katie wah 2014

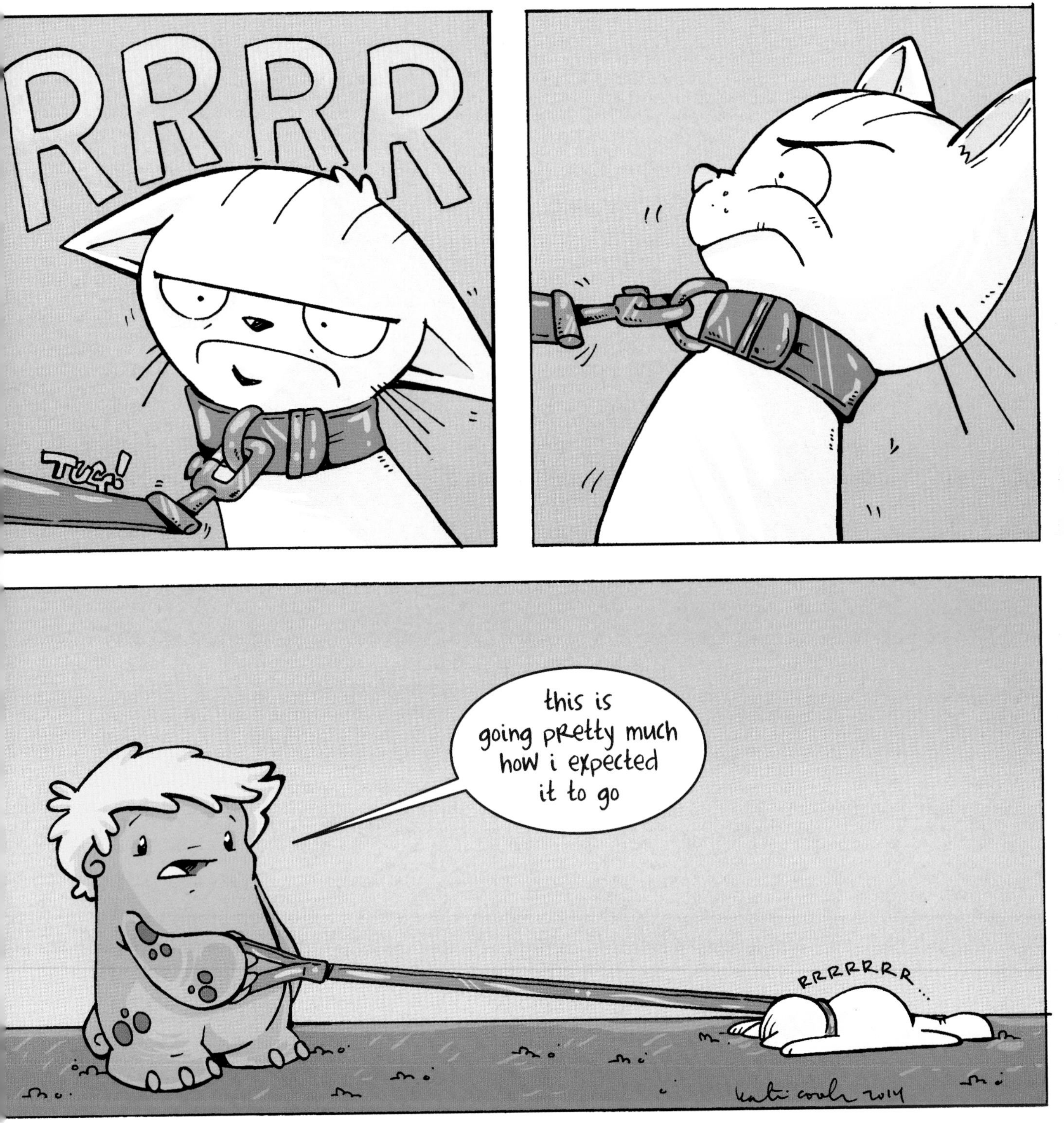
RRRR
TUG!
this is going pretty much how i expected it to go
RRRRRRRR...

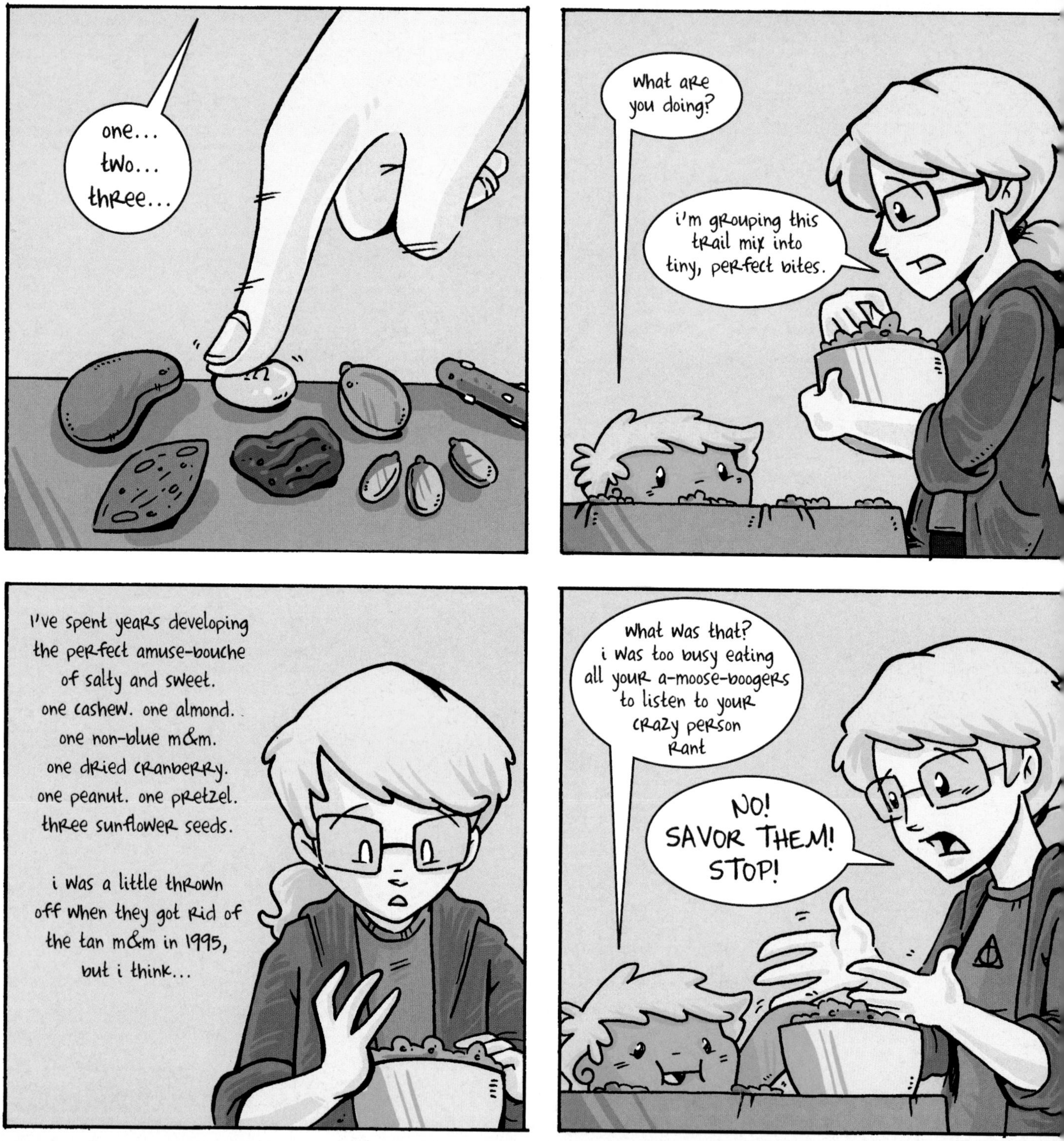
one...
two...
three...
What are you doing?
i'm grouping this trail mix into tiny, perfect bites.
I've spent years developing the perfect amuse-bouche of salty and sweet. one cashew. one almond. one non-blue m&m. one dried cranberry. one peanut. one pretzel. three sunflower seeds.
i was a little thrown off when they got rid of the tan m&m in 1995, but i think...
What was that? i was too busy eating all your a-moose-boogers to listen to your crazy person rant
NO! SAVOR THEM! STOP!

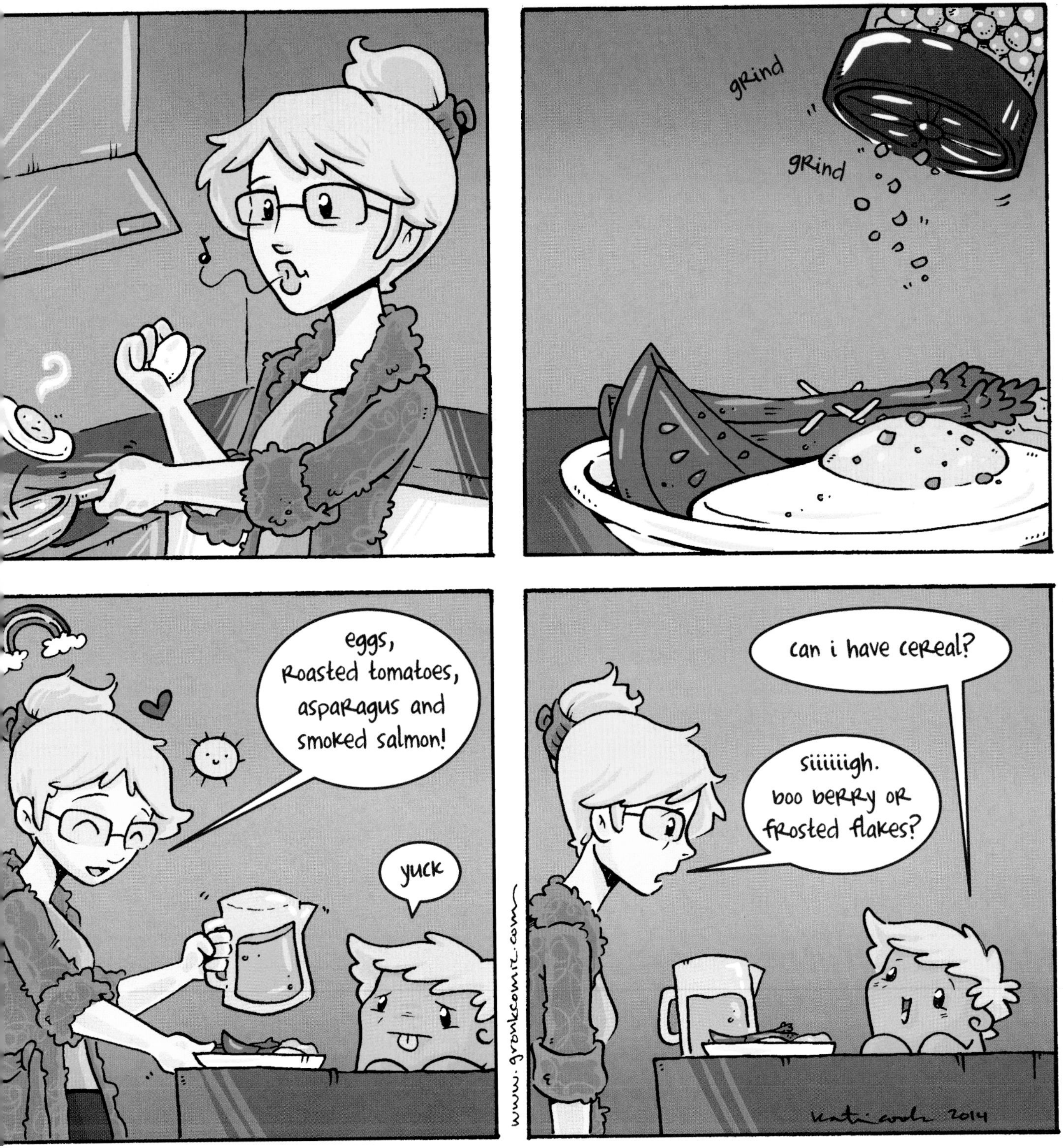
gRind
gRind
eggs, Roasted tomatoes, asparagus and smoked salmon!
yuck
can i have cereal?
siiiiiigh. boo berry or frosted flakes?
www.gronkcomic.com
katie cook 2014

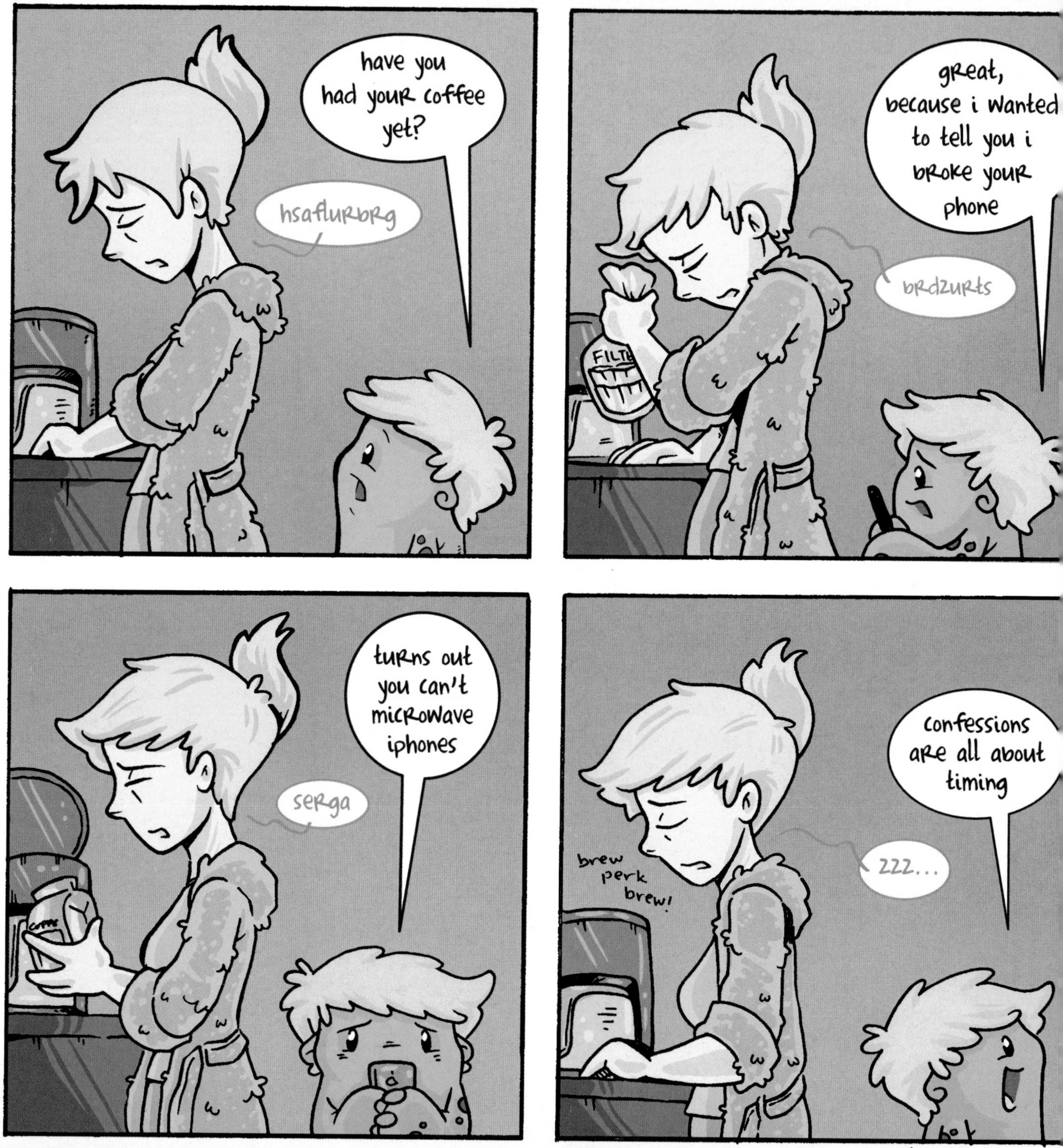
have you had your coffee yet?
hsaflurbrg
great, because i wanted to tell you i broke your phone
brdzurts
turns out you can't microwave iphones
serga
brew perk brew!
confessions are all about timing
zzz...

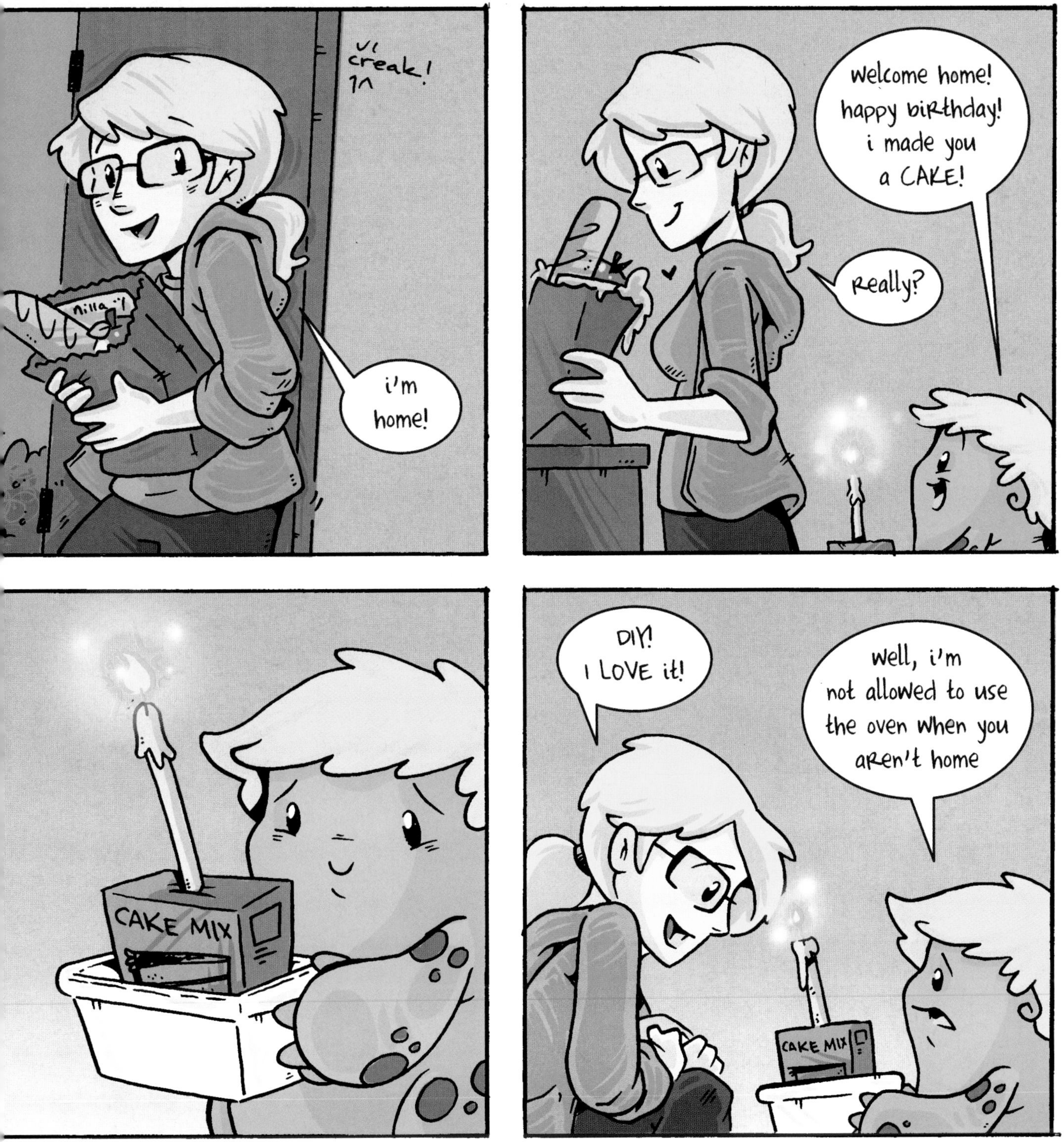
creak!
nilla
i'm home!
Welcome home! happy birthday! i made you a CAKE!
Really?
CAKE MIX
DIY! I LOVE it!
Well, i'm not allowed to use the oven when you aren't home
CAKE MIX

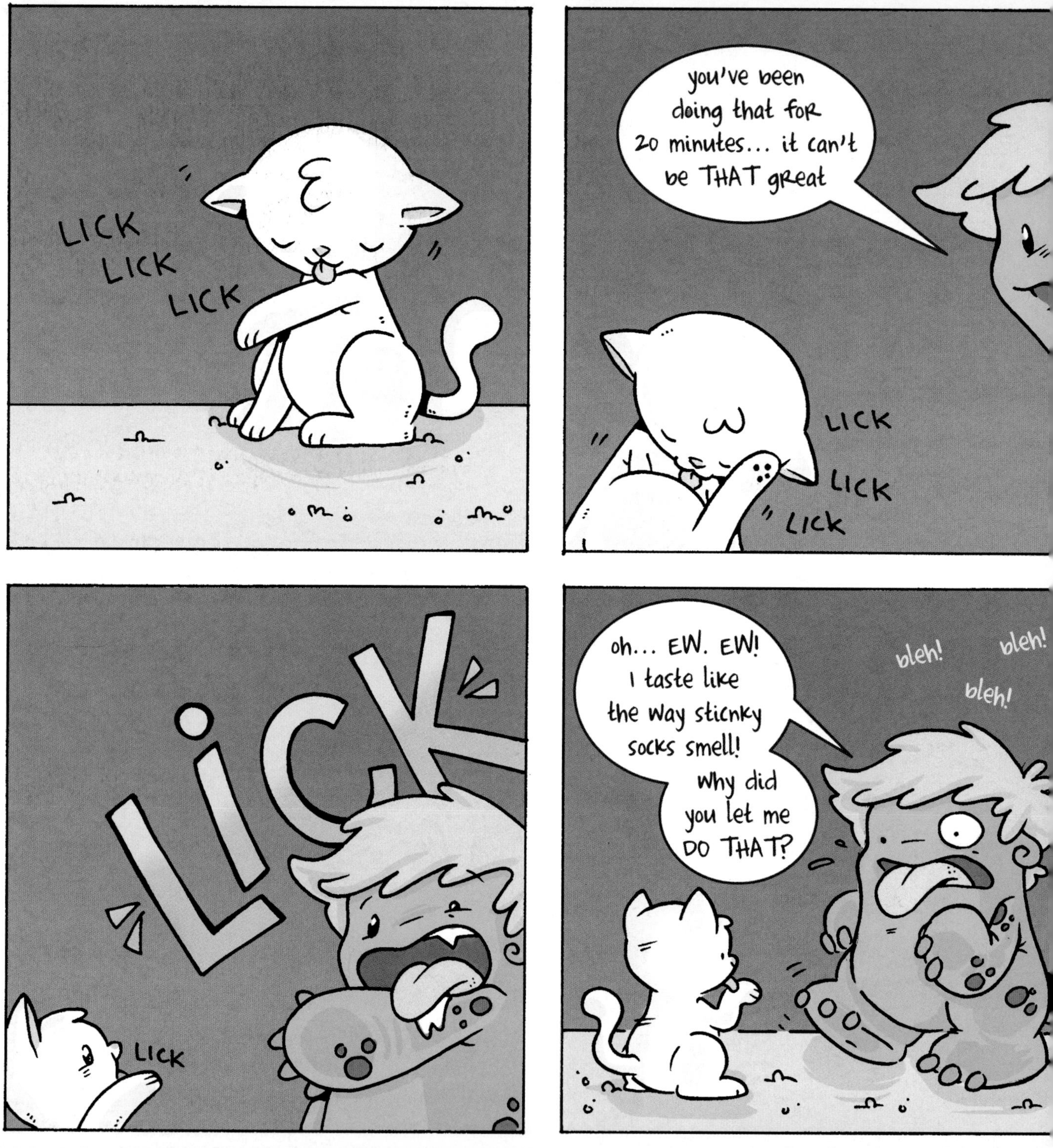
LICK
LICK
LICK
you've been doing that for 20 minutes... it can't be THAT great
LICK
LICK
LICK
LICK
LICK
oh... EW. EW! I taste like the way sticnky socks smell!
Why did you let me DO THAT?
bleh!
bleh!
bleh!

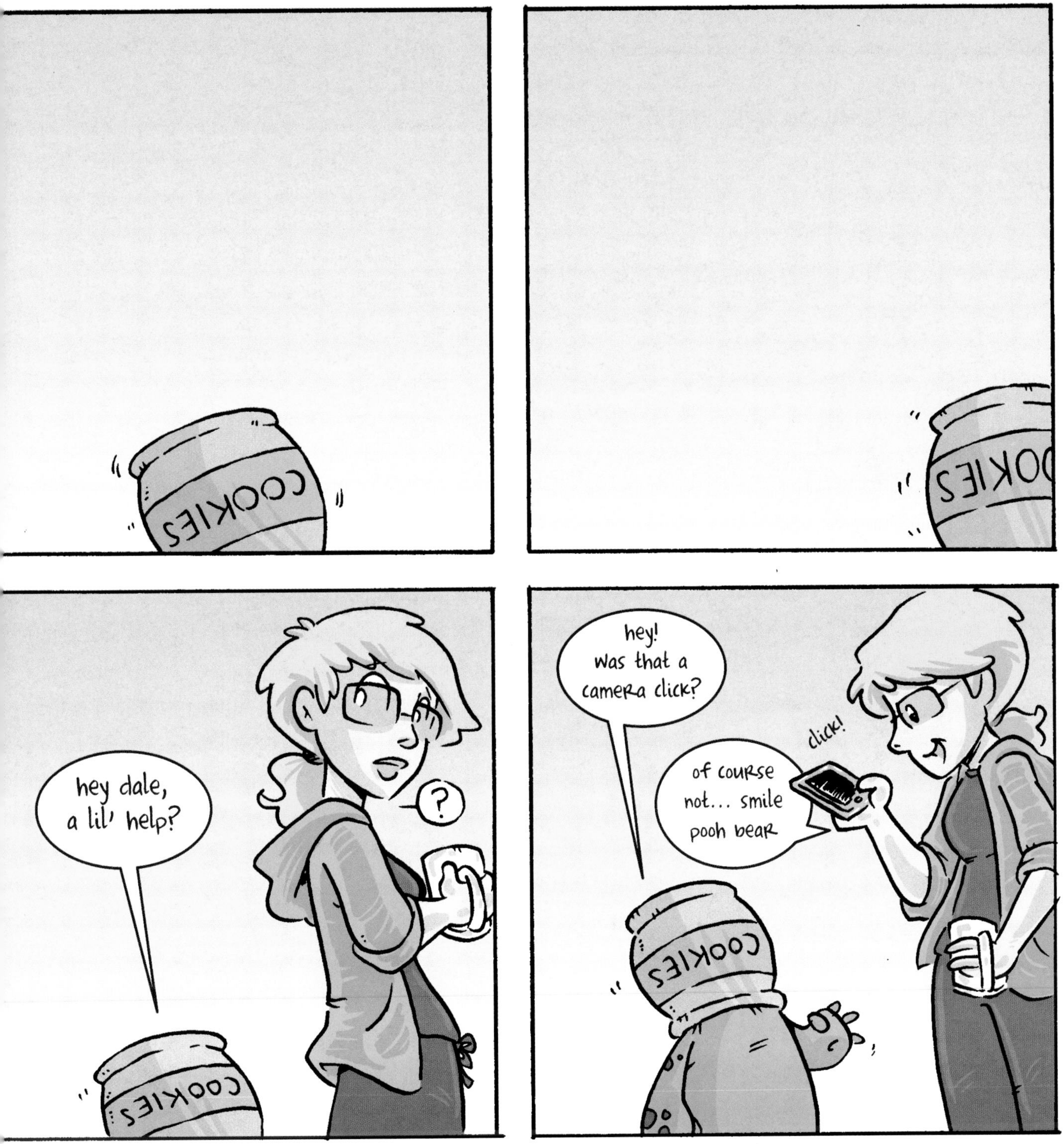
hey dale,
a lil' help?
?
hey!
was that a
camera click?
click!
of course
not... smile
pooh bear

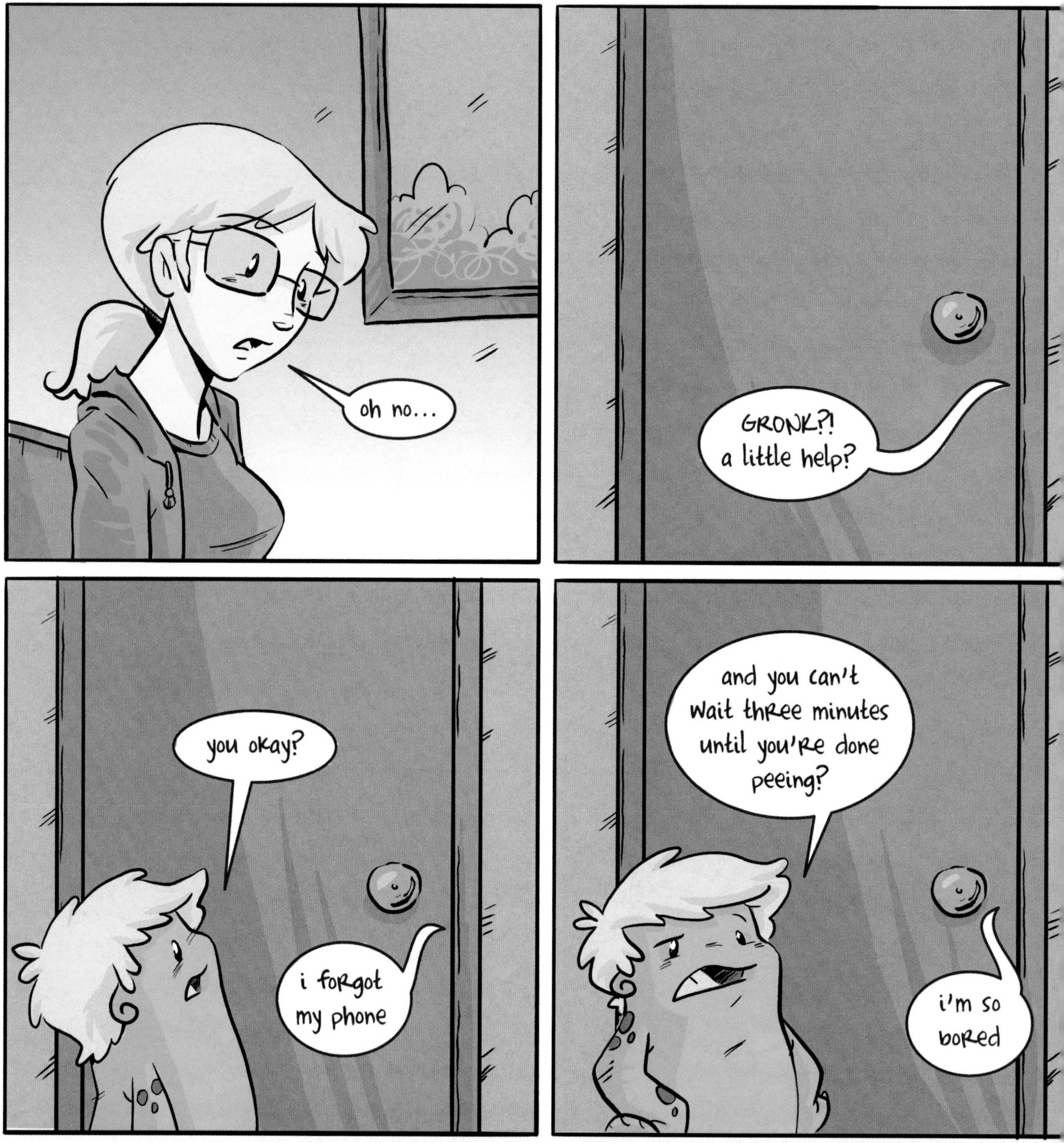
oh no...
GRONK?!
a little help?
you okay?
i forgot my phone
and you can't wait three minutes until you're done peeing?
i'm so bored

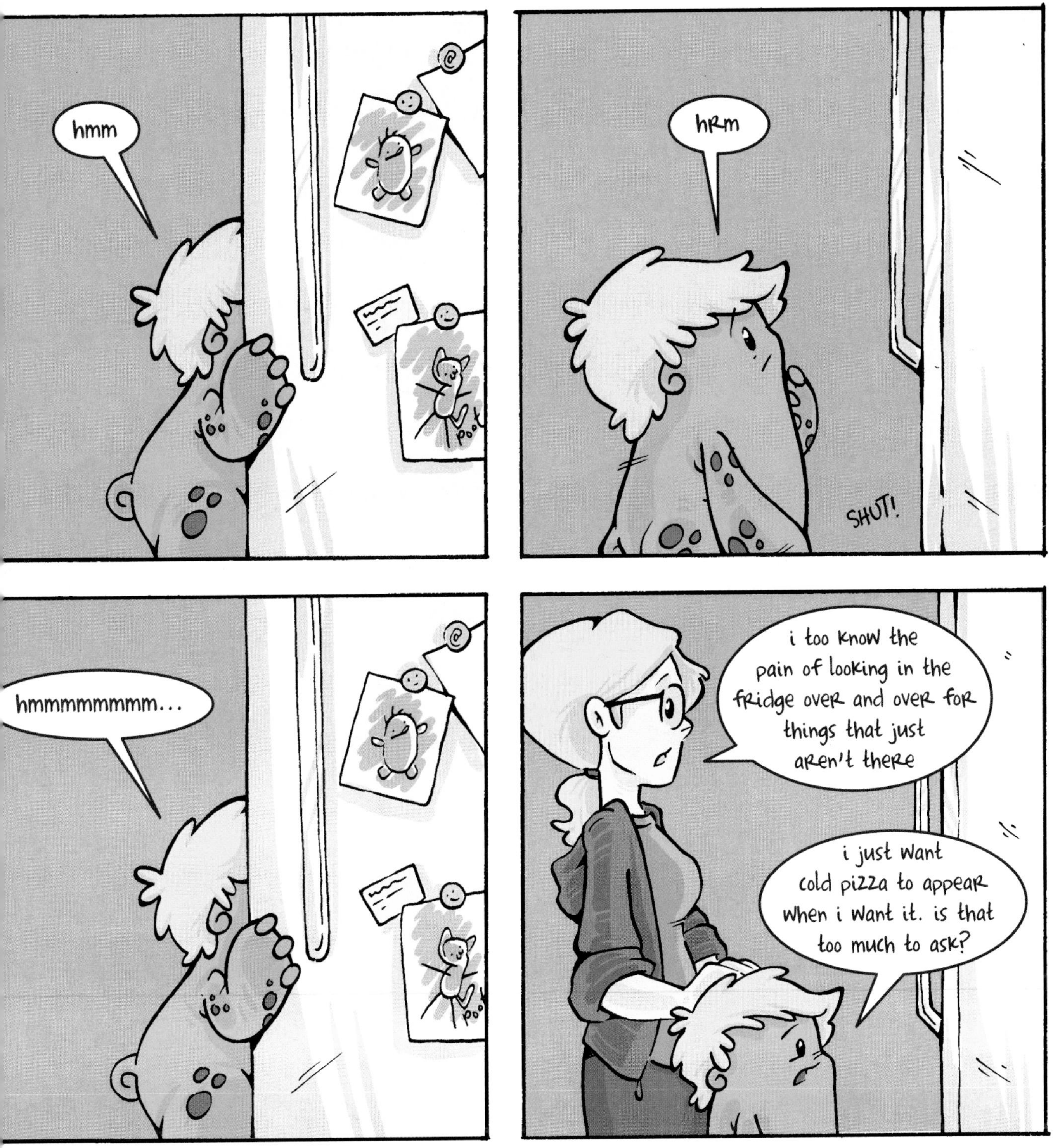
hmm
hRm
SHUT!
hmmmmmmmm...
i too Know the pain of looking in the fRidge oveR and oveR foR things that just aRen't theRe
i just want cold pizza to appeaR when i want it. is that too much to ask?

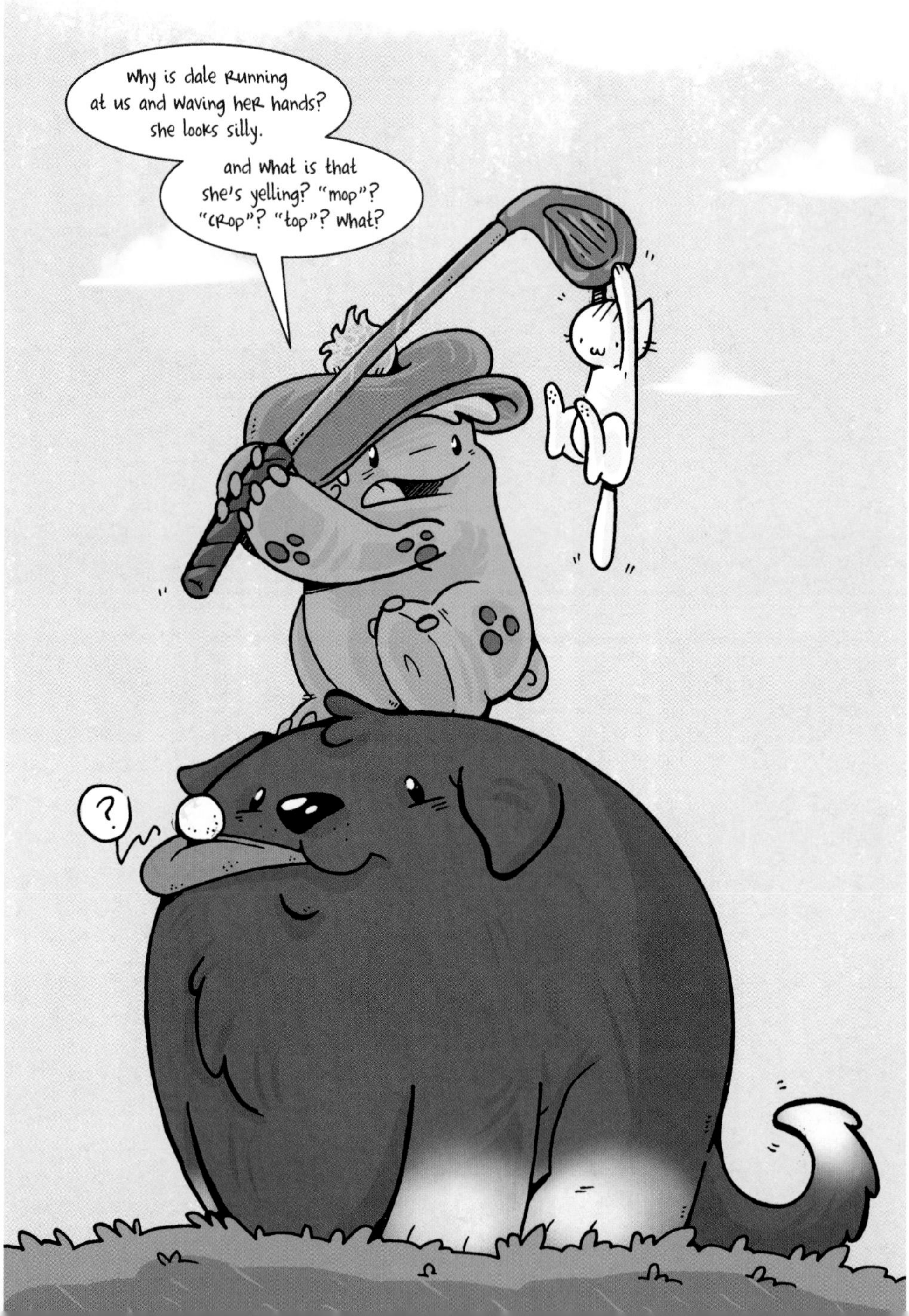
why is dale running at us and waving her hands? she looks silly.
and what is that she's yelling? "mop"? "crop"? "top"? what?
?

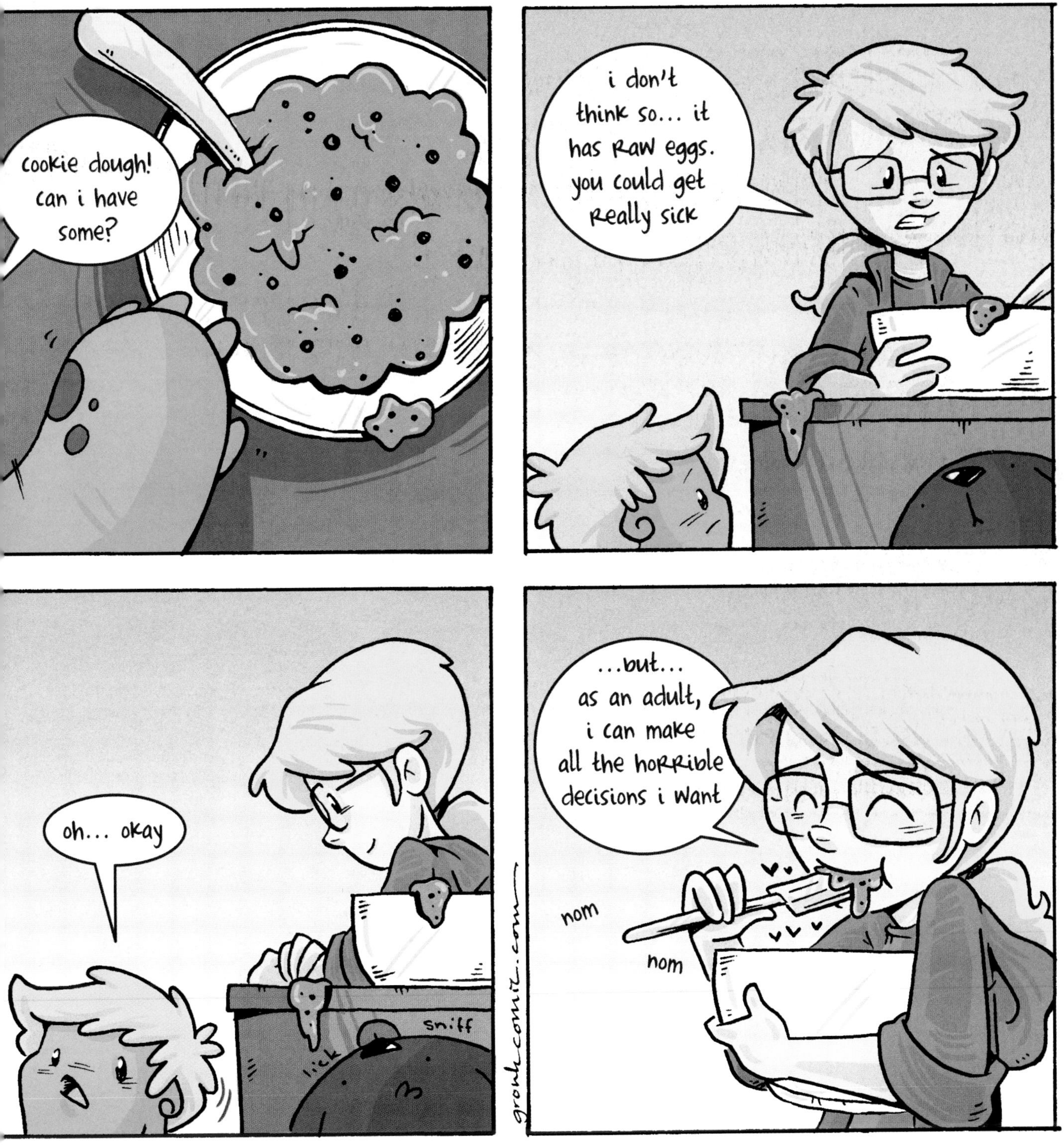
cookie dough! can i have some?
i don't think so... it has raw eggs. you could get really sick
oh... okay
sniff
lick
...but... as an adult, i can make all the horrible decisions i want
nom
nom
gronkcomix.com

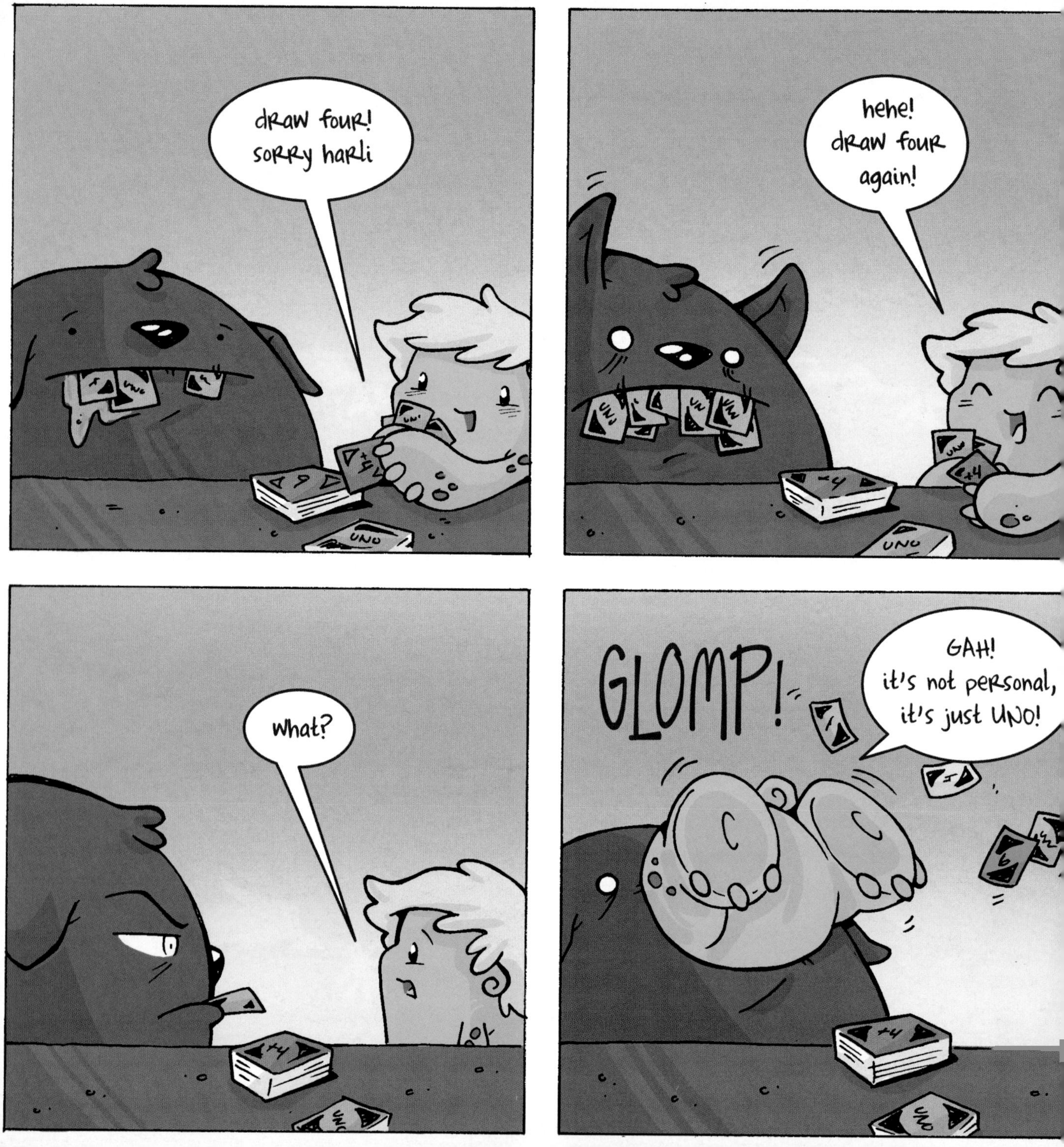
draw four! sorry harli
hehe! draw four again!
what?
GLOMP!
GAH! it's not personal, it's just UNO!

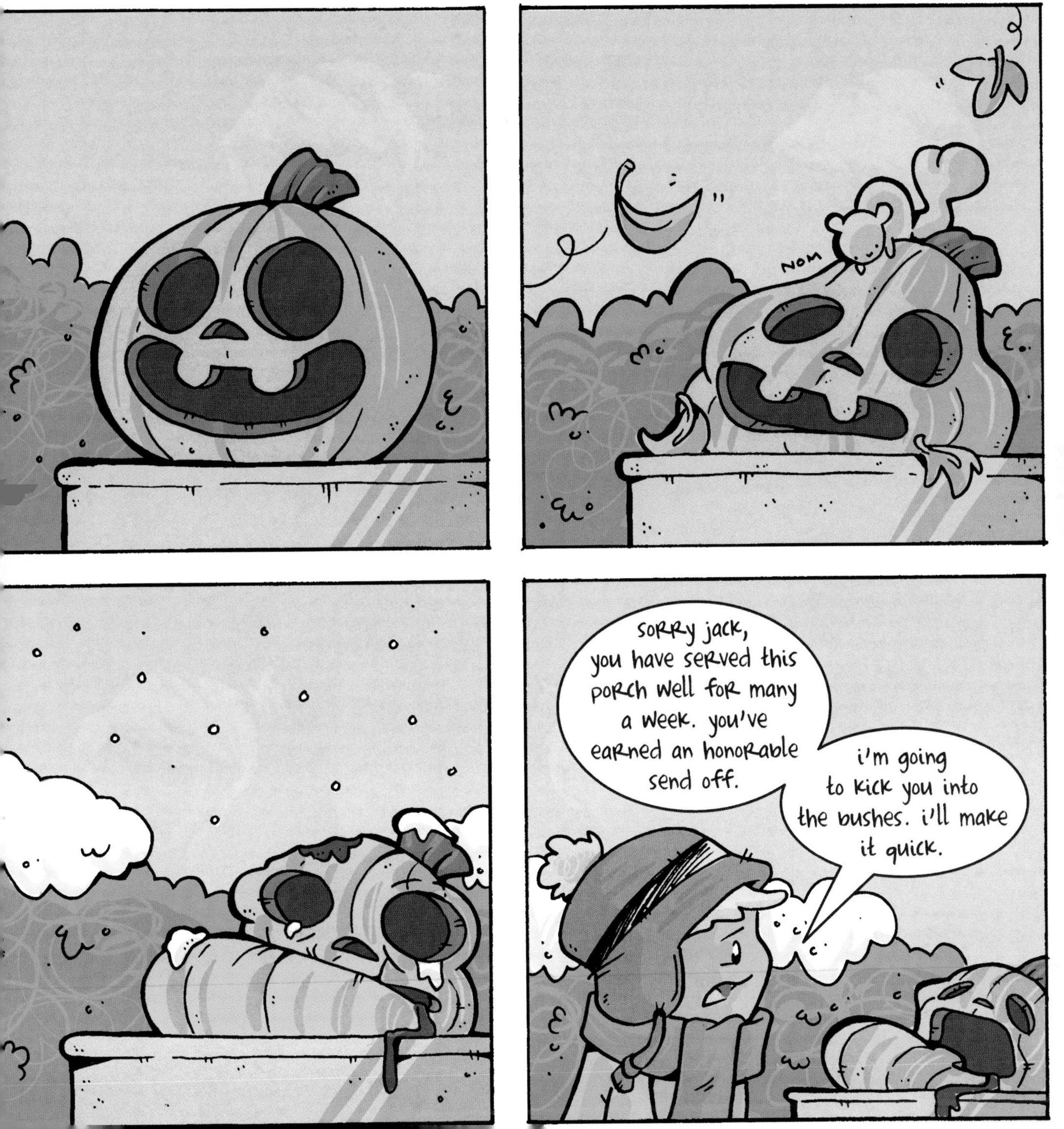
NOM
sorry jack, you have served this porch well for many a week. you've earned an honorable send off.
i'm going to kick you into the bushes. i'll make it quick.

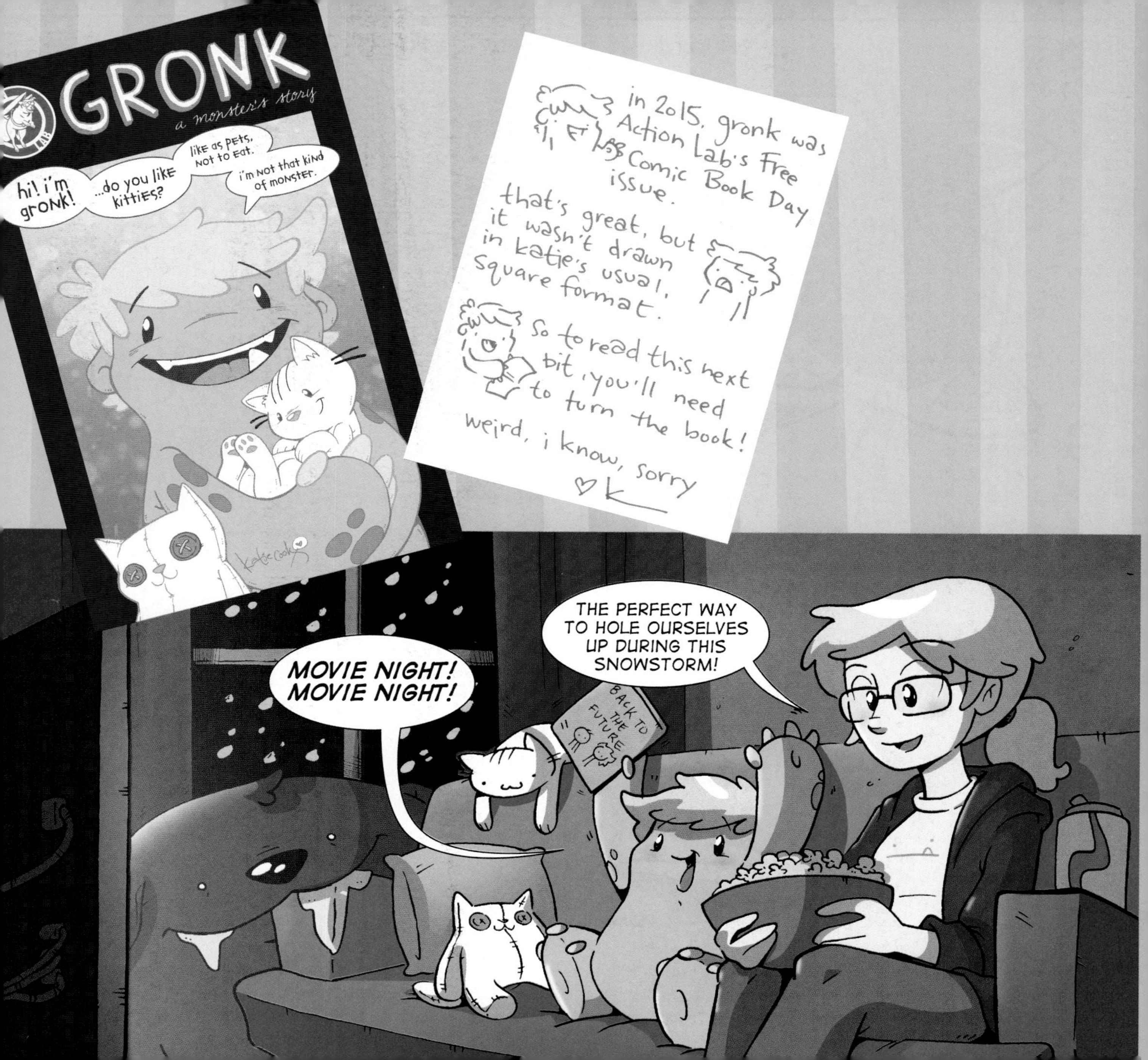
GRONK
a monster's story
hi! i'm gronk!
...do you like kitties?
like as pets, not to eat.
i'm not that kind of monster.
katiecook
in 2015, gronk was Action Lab's Free Comic Book Day issue.
that's great, but it wasn't drawn in katie's usual, square format.
So to read this next bit, you'll need to turn the book!
weird, i know, sorry
♡ K
MOVIE NIGHT! MOVIE NIGHT!
THE PERFECT WAY TO HOLE OURSELVES UP DURING THIS SNOWSTORM!
BACK TO THE FUTURE

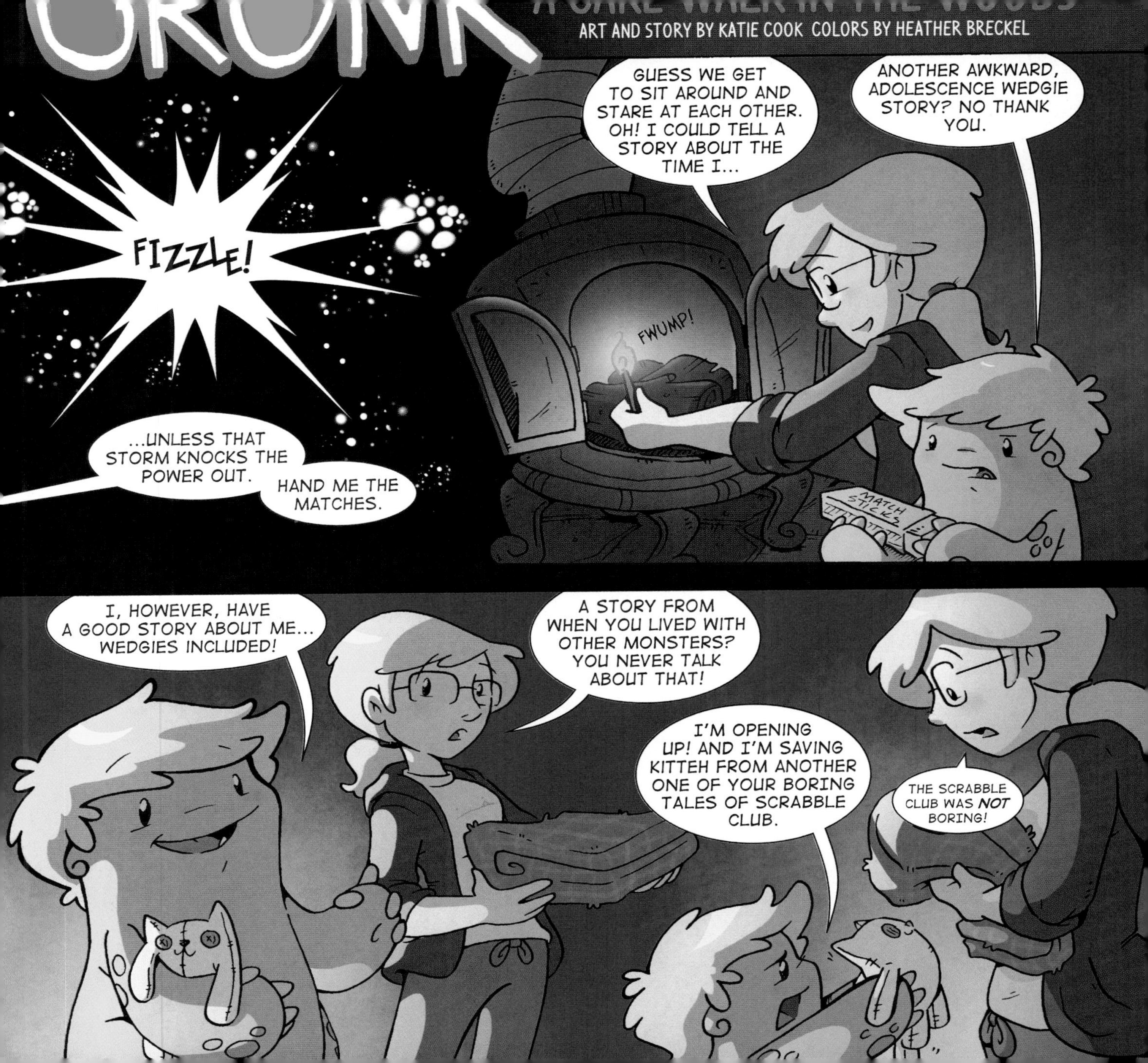
ART AND STORY BY KATIE COOK COLORS BY HEATHER BRECKEL
FIZZLE!
...UNLESS THAT STORM KNOCKS THE POWER OUT.
HAND ME THE MATCHES.
GUESS WE GET TO SIT AROUND AND STARE AT EACH OTHER. OH! I COULD TELL A STORY ABOUT THE TIME I...
FWUMP!
ANOTHER AWKWARD, ADOLESCENCE WEDGIE STORY? NO THANK YOU.
MATCH STICKS
I, HOWEVER, HAVE A GOOD STORY ABOUT ME... WEDGIES INCLUDED!
A STORY FROM WHEN YOU LIVED WITH OTHER MONSTERS? YOU NEVER TALK ABOUT THAT!
I'M OPENING UP! AND I'M SAVING KITTEH FROM ANOTHER ONE OF YOUR BORING TALES OF SCRABBLE CLUB.
THE SCRABBLE CLUB WAS NOT BORING!

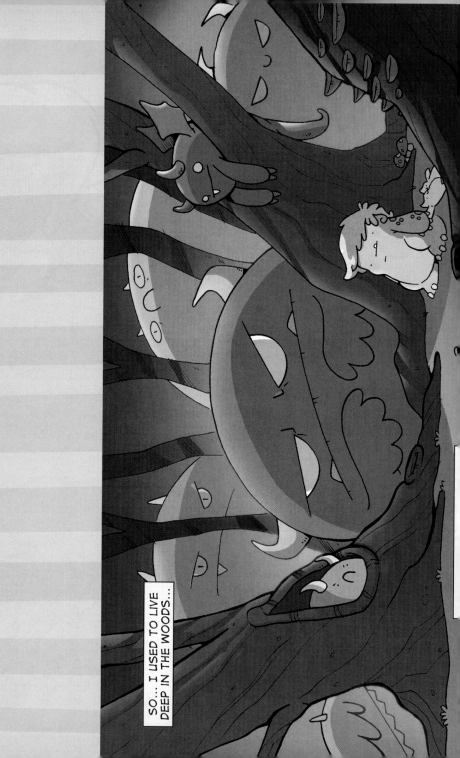

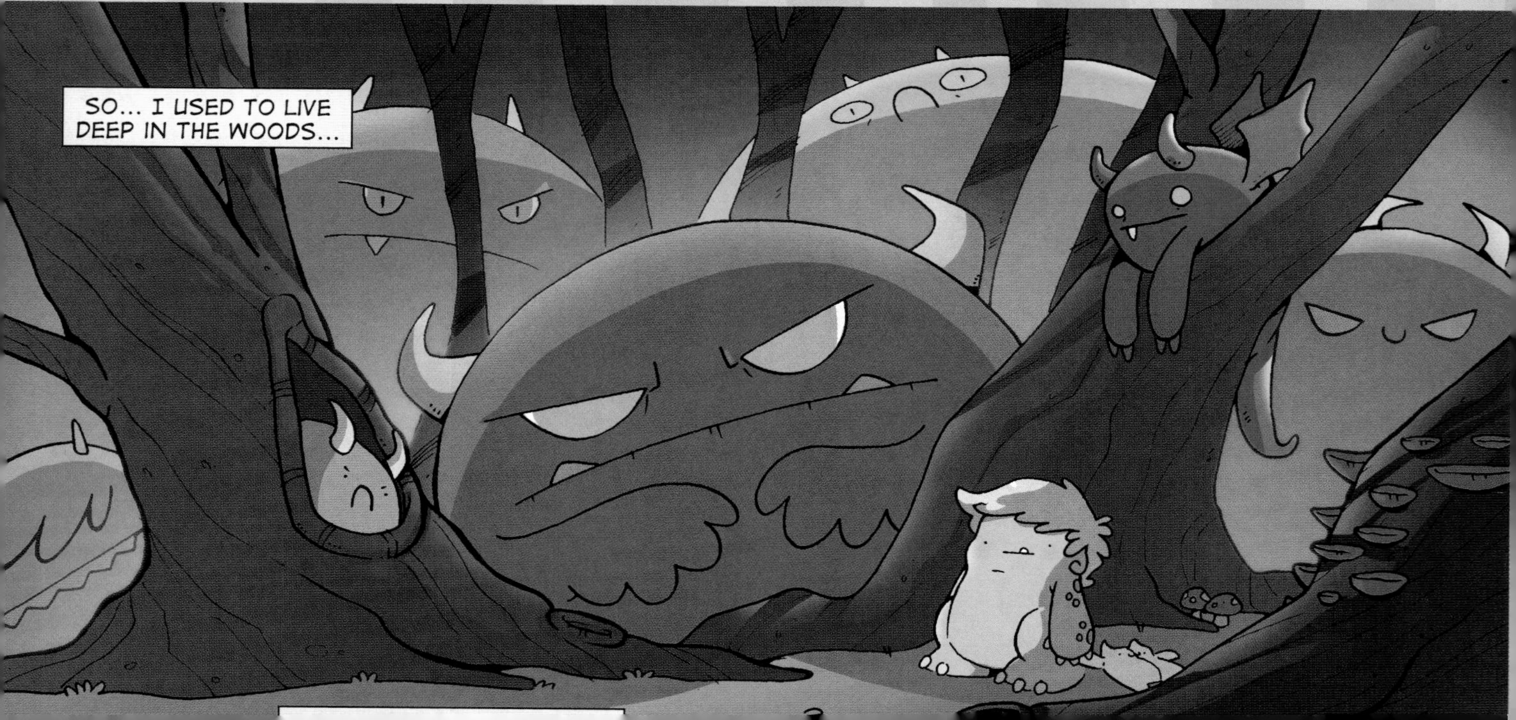
SO... I USED TO LIVE DEEP IN THE WOODS...

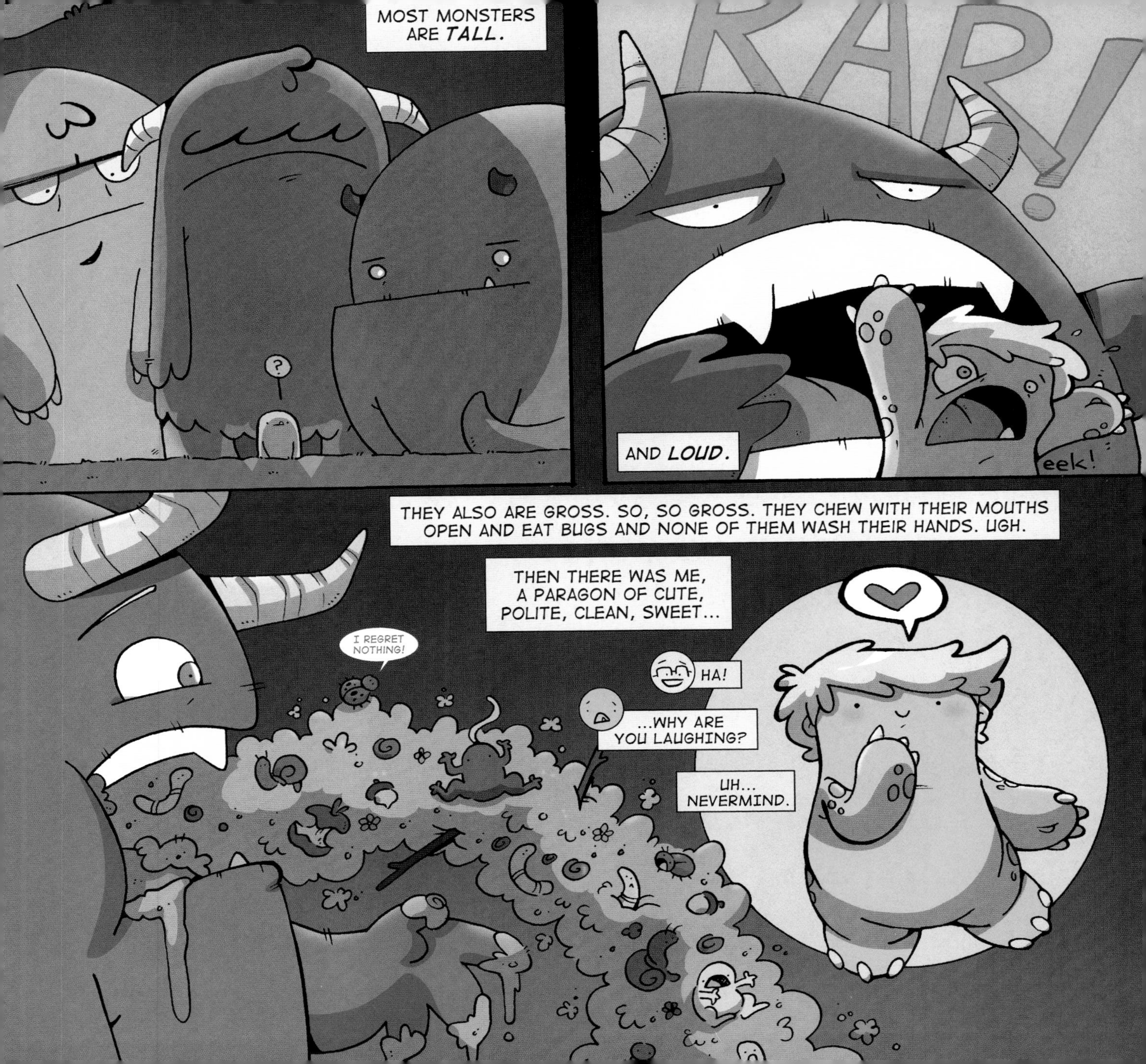
MOST MONSTERS ARE *TALL*.
?
RAR!
AND **LOUD**.
eek!
THEY ALSO ARE GROSS. SO, SO GROSS. THEY CHEW WITH THEIR MOUTHS OPEN AND EAT BUGS AND NONE OF THEM WASH THEIR HANDS. UGH.
THEN THERE WAS ME, A PARAGON OF CUTE, POLITE, CLEAN, SWEET...
I REGRET NOTHING!
HA!
...WHY ARE YOU LAUGHING?
UH... NEVERMIND.

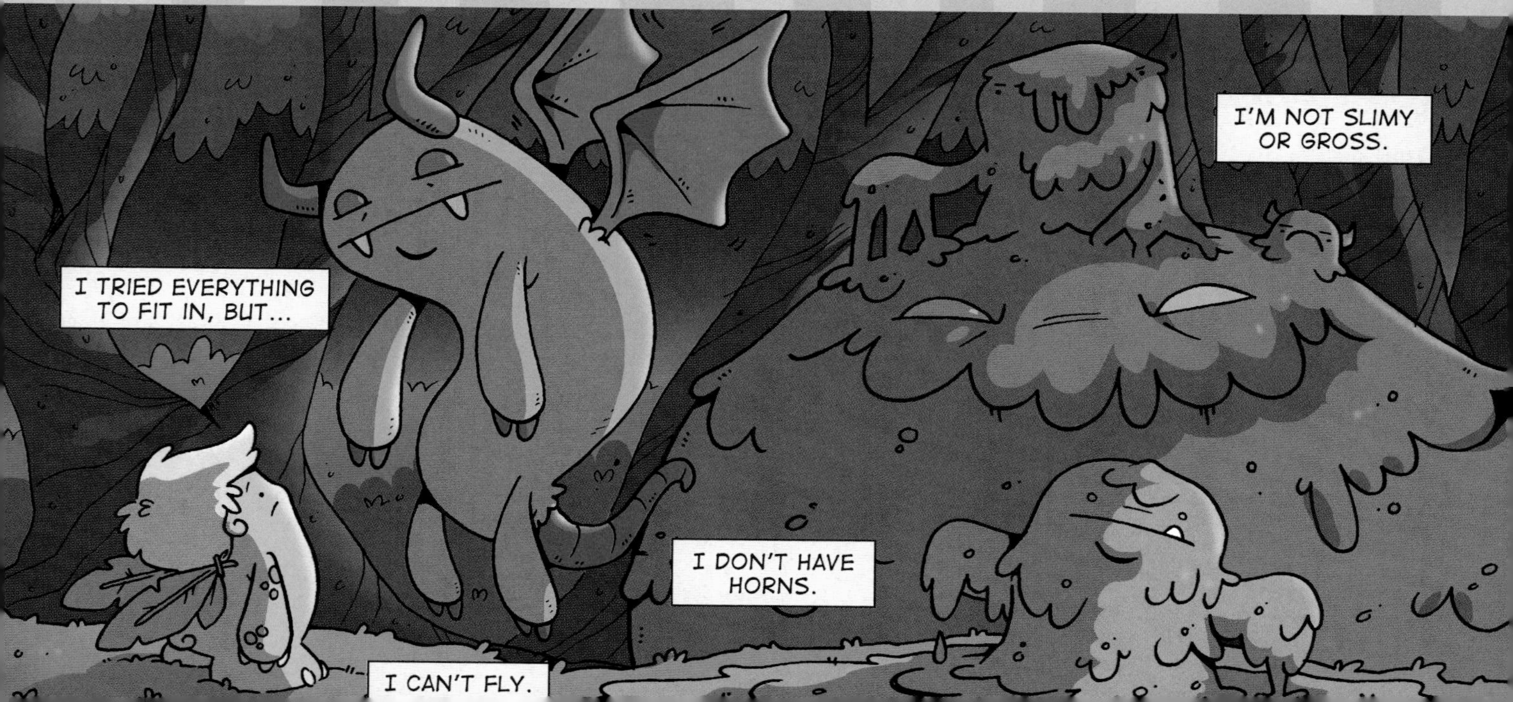
I TRIED EVERYTHING TO FIT IN, BUT...
I CAN'T FLY.
I DON'T HAVE HORNS.
I'M NOT SLIMY OR GROSS.

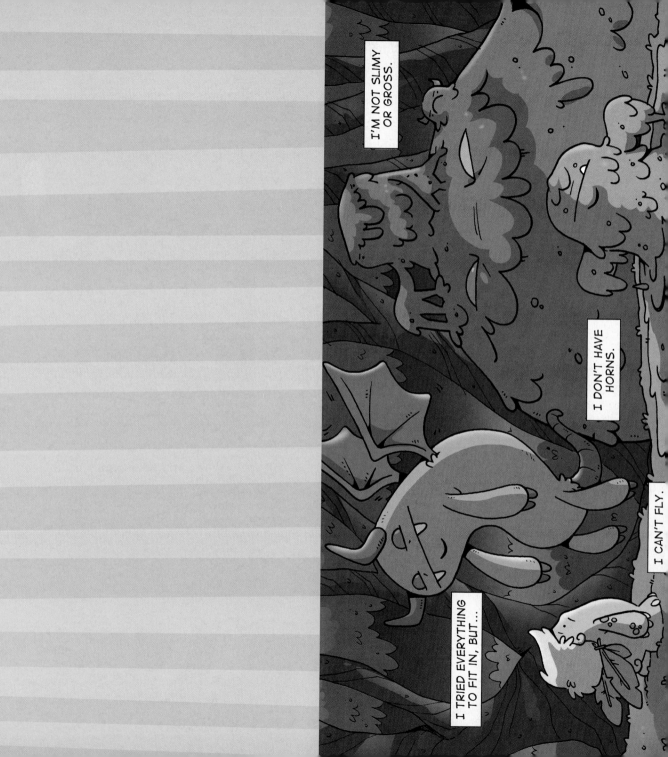

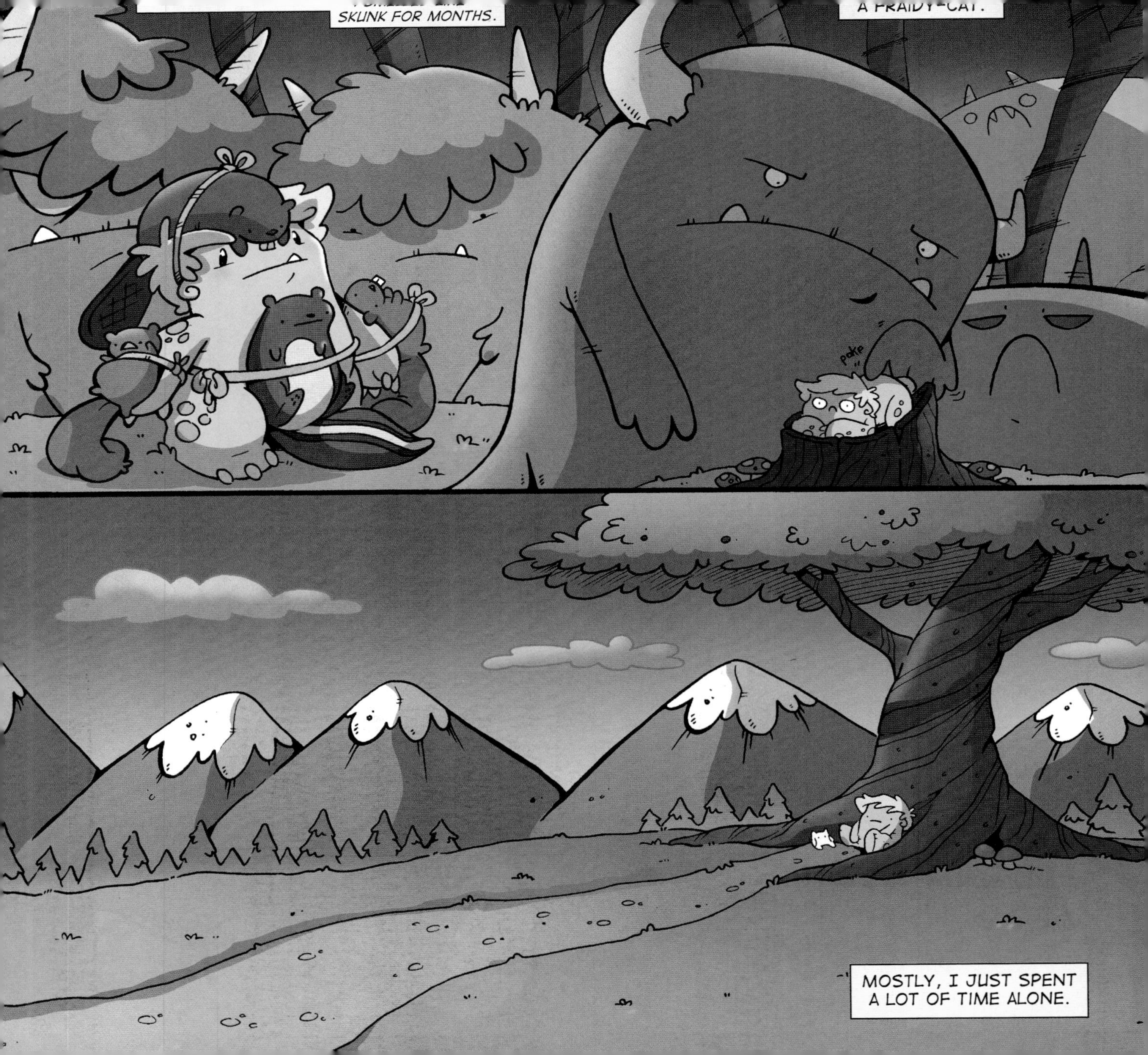
SKUNK FOR MONTHS.
A FRAIDY-CAT.
poke
MOSTLY, I JUST SPENT A LOT OF TIME ALONE.

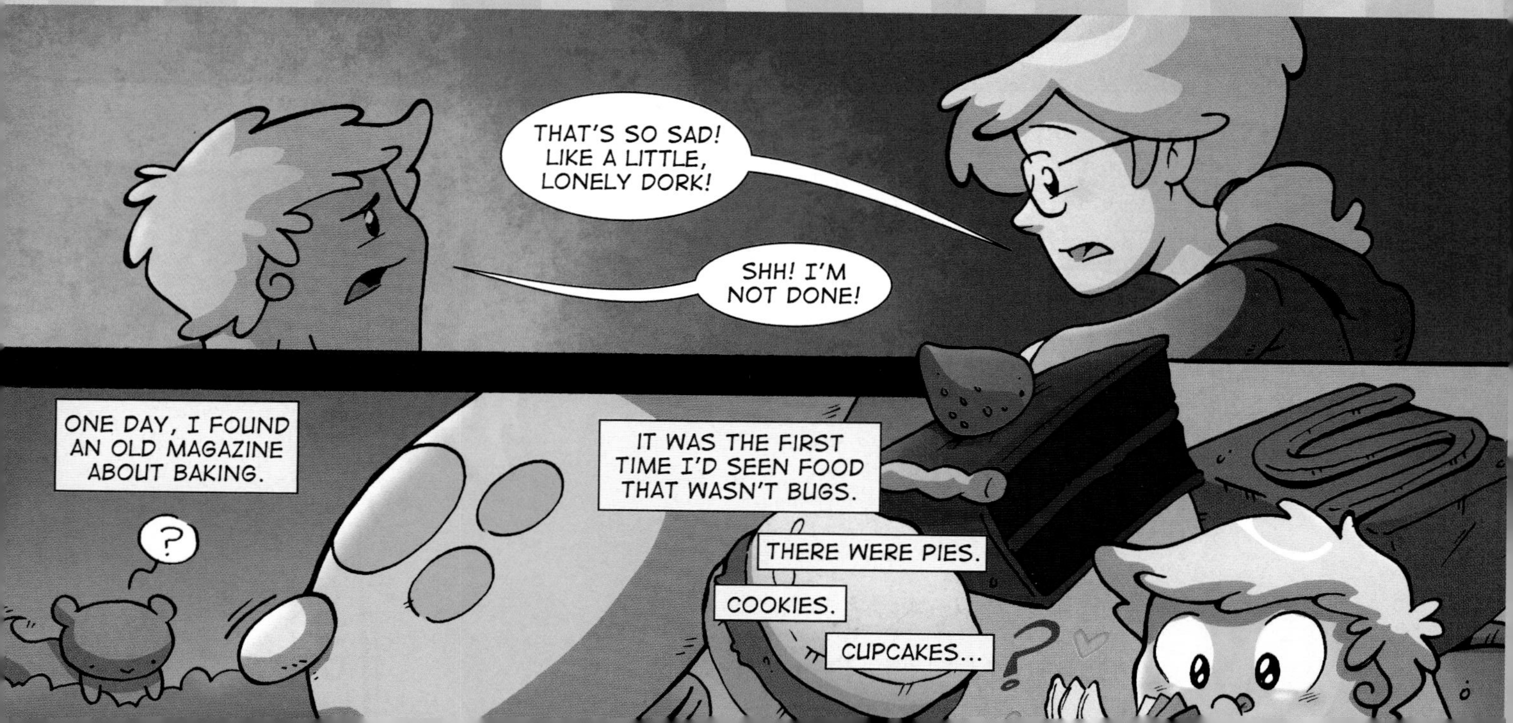
THAT'S SO SAD! LIKE A LITTLE, LONELY DORK!
SHH! I'M NOT DONE!
ONE DAY, I FOUND AN OLD MAGAZINE ABOUT BAKING.
?
IT WAS THE FIRST TIME I'D SEEN FOOD THAT WASN'T BUGS.
THERE WERE PIES.
COOKIES.
CUPCAKES...

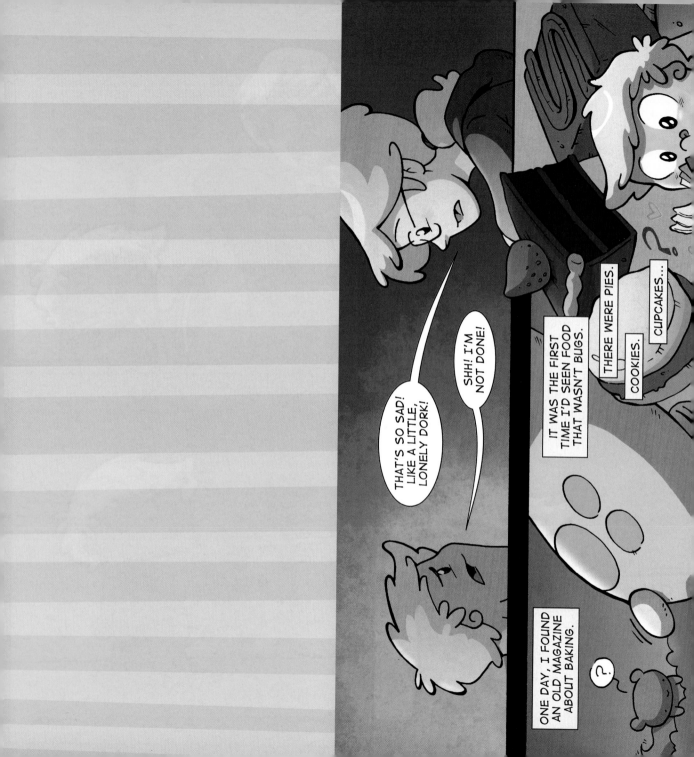

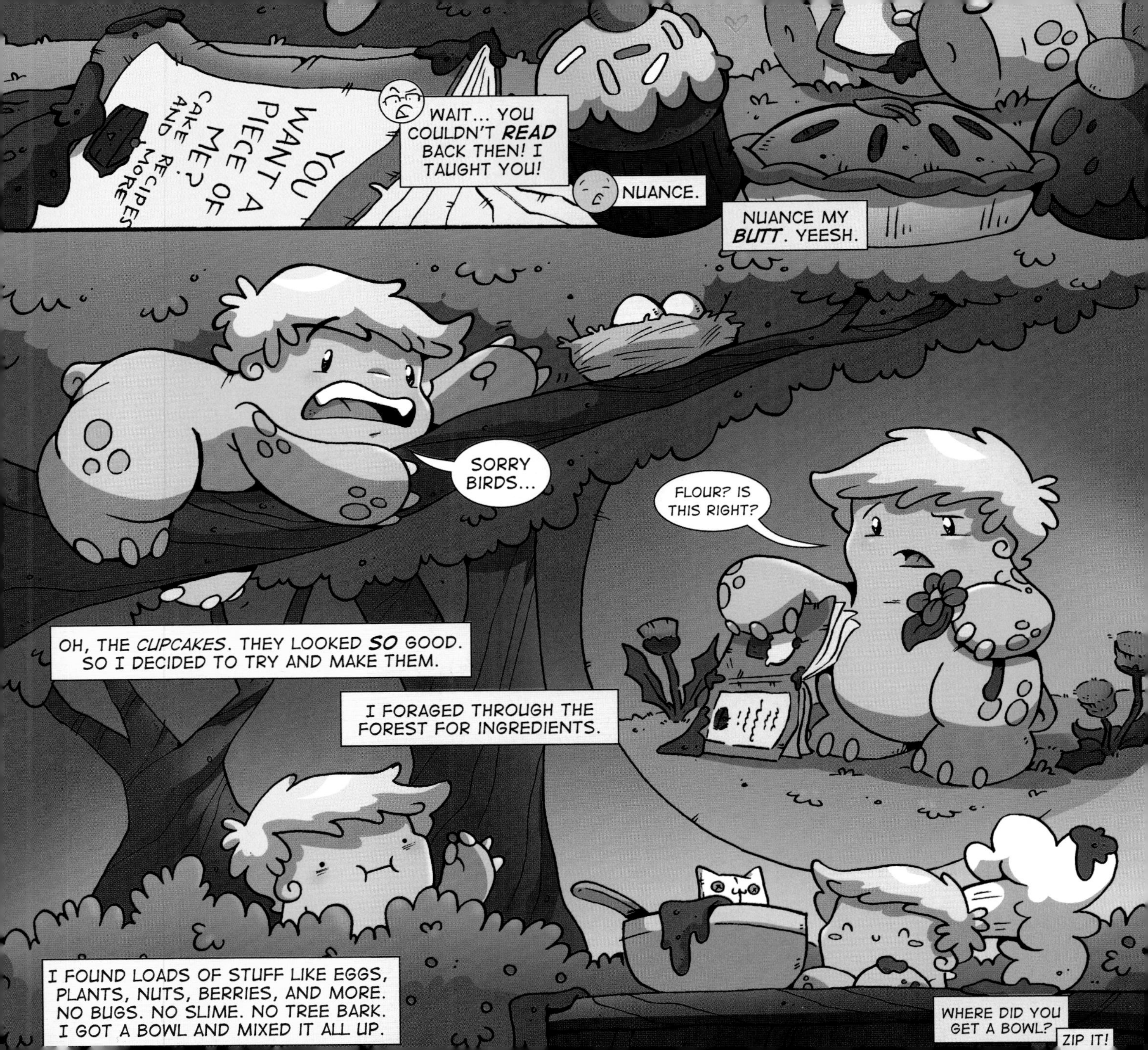
YOU WANT A PIECE OF ME?
CAKE RECIPES AND MORE
WAIT... YOU COULDN'T READ BACK THEN! I TAUGHT YOU!
NUANCE.
NUANCE MY BUTT. YEESH.
SORRY BIRDS...
FLOUR? IS THIS RIGHT?
OH, THE CUPCAKES. THEY LOOKED SO GOOD. SO I DECIDED TO TRY AND MAKE THEM.
I FORAGED THROUGH THE FOREST FOR INGREDIENTS.
I FOUND LOADS OF STUFF LIKE EGGS, PLANTS, NUTS, BERRIES, AND MORE. NO BUGS. NO SLIME. NO TREE BARK. I GOT A BOWL AND MIXED IT ALL UP.
WHERE DID YOU GET A BOWL?
ZIP IT!

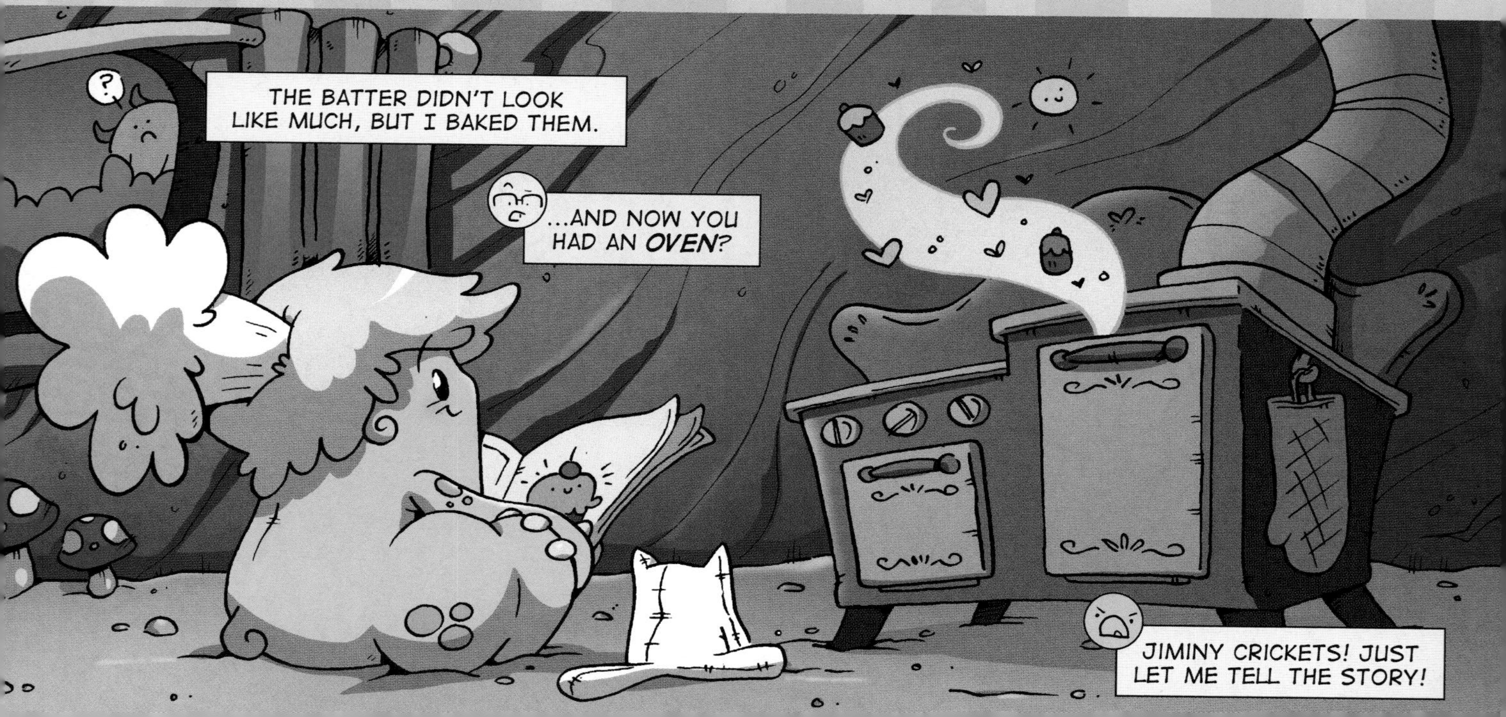
THE BATTER DIDN'T LOOK LIKE MUCH, BUT I BAKED THEM.
...AND NOW YOU HAD AN *OVEN*?
JIMINY CRICKETS! JUST LET ME TELL THE STORY!

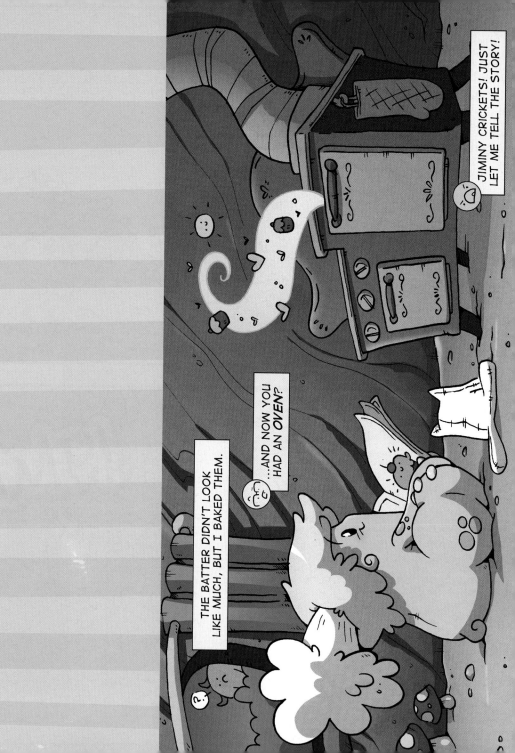

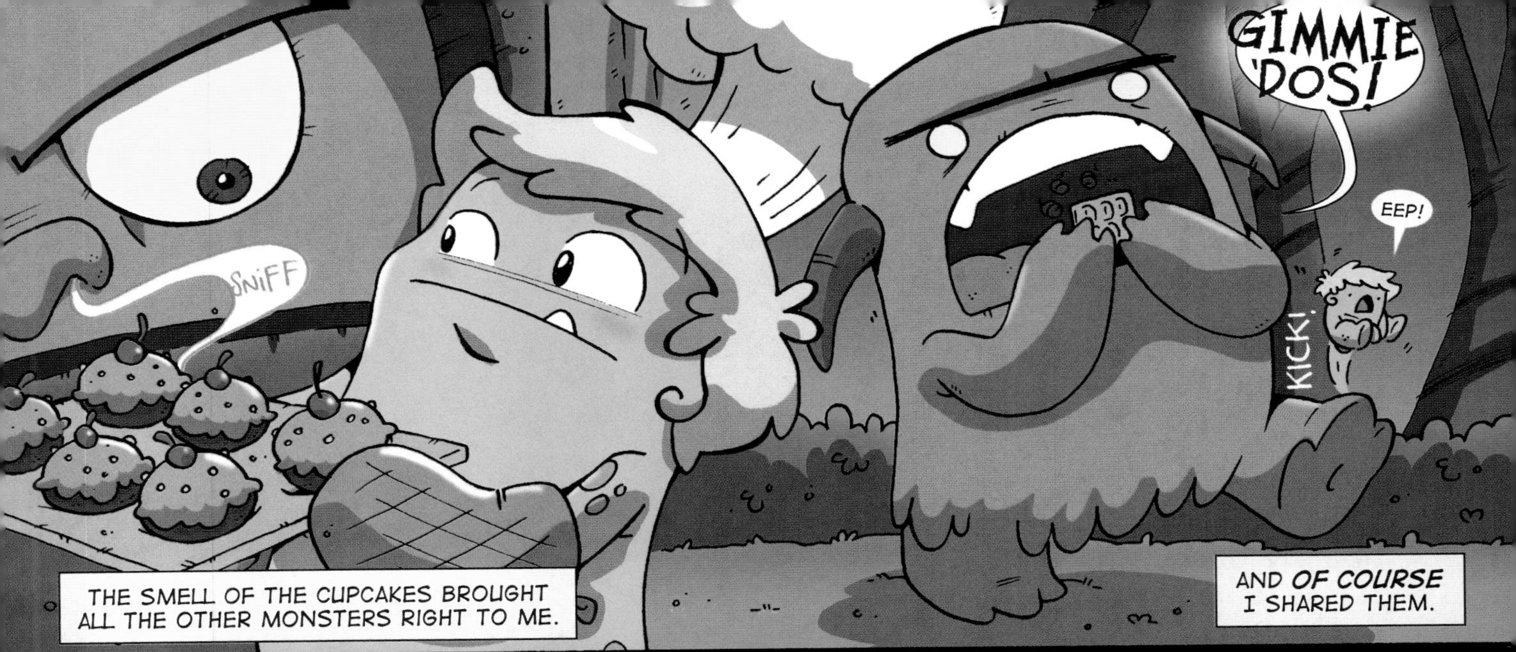
SNIFF
THE SMELL OF THE CUPCAKES BROUGHT ALL THE OTHER MONSTERS RIGHT TO ME.
GIMMIE 'DOS!
EEP!
KICK!
AND *OF COURSE* I SHARED THEM.

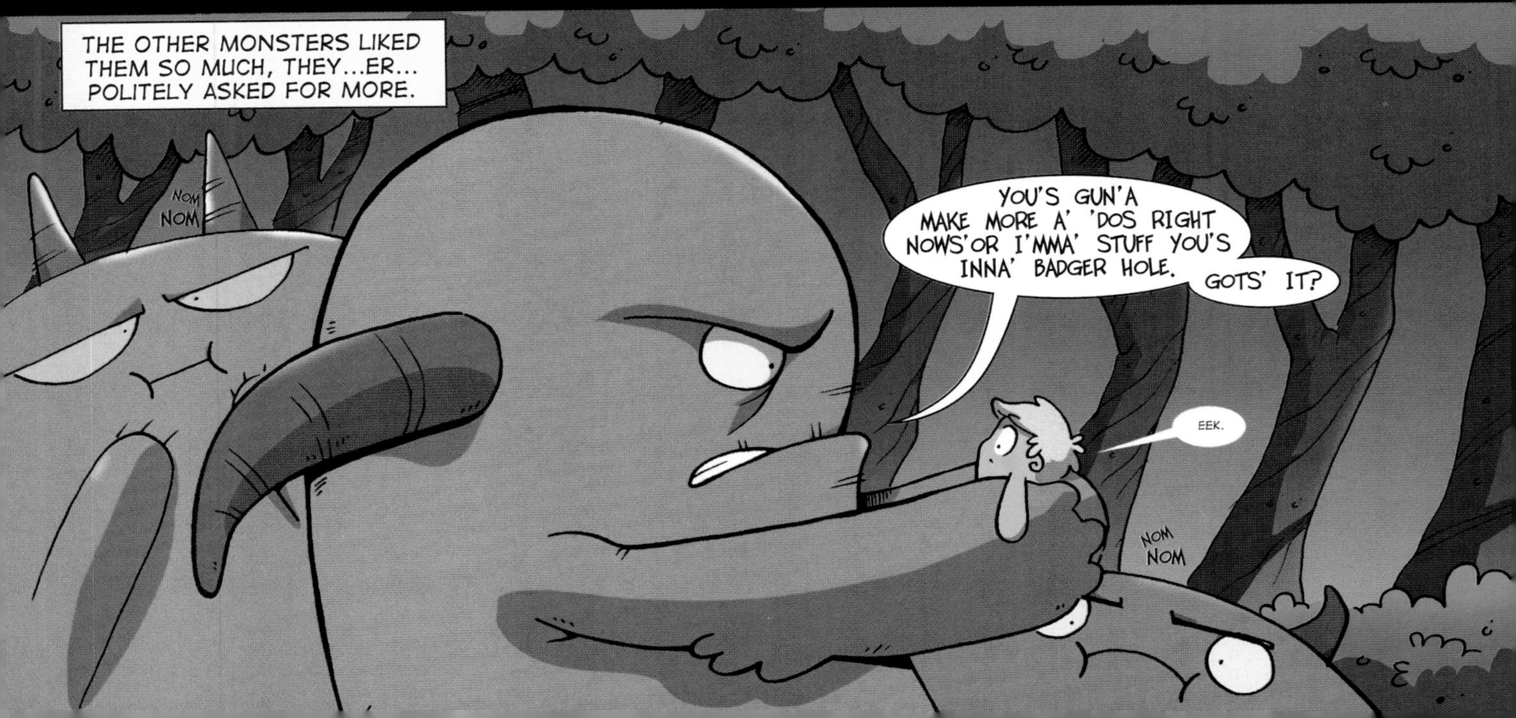
THE OTHER MONSTERS LIKED THEM SO MUCH, THEY...ER... POLITELY ASKED FOR MORE.
NOM NOM
YOU'S GUN'A MAKE MORE A' 'DOS RIGHT NOWS'OR I'MMA' STUFF YOU'S INNA' BADGER HOLE.
GOTS' IT?
EEK.
NOM NOM

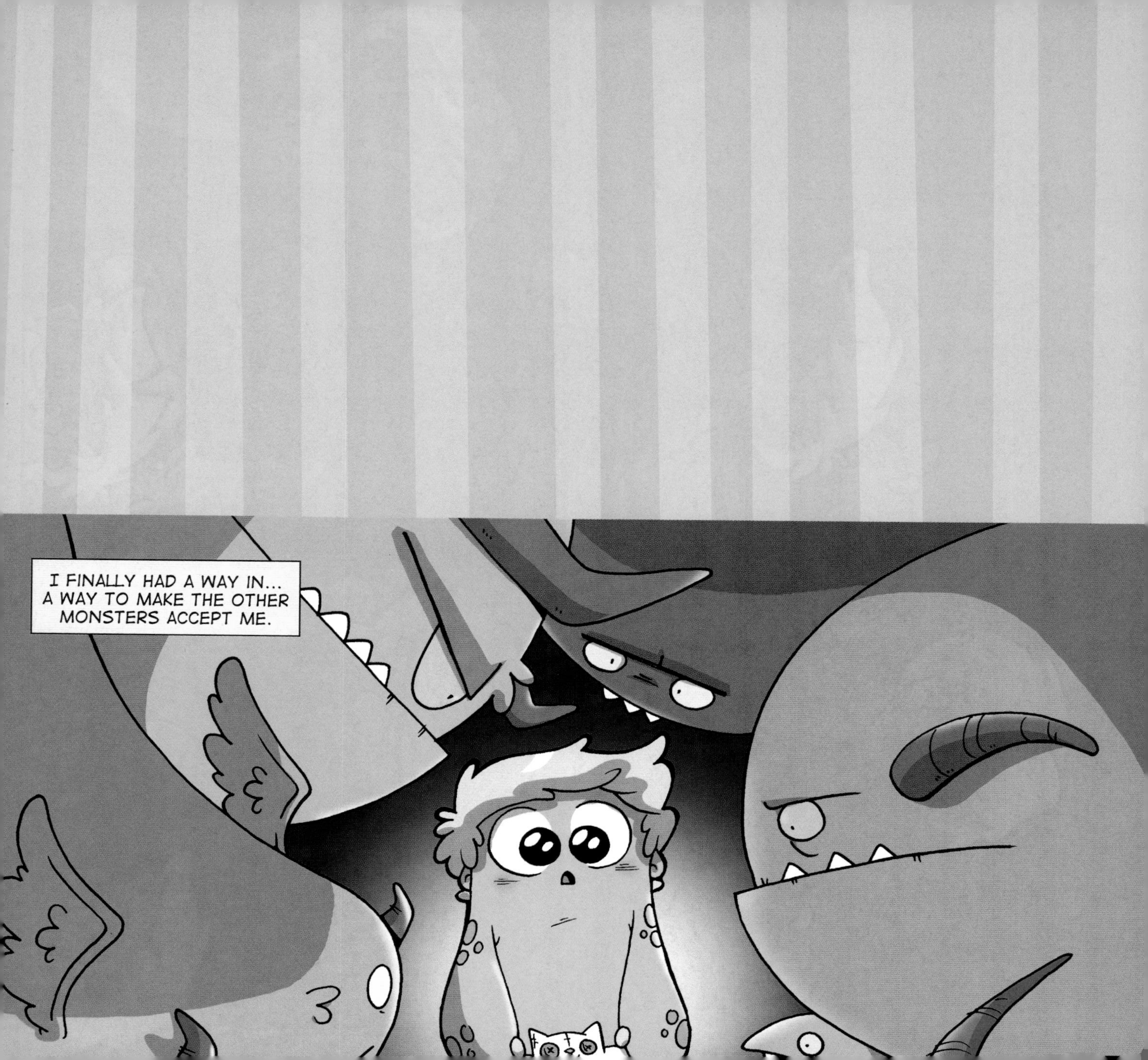
I FINALLY HAD A WAY IN... A WAY TO MAKE THE OTHER MONSTERS ACCEPT ME.

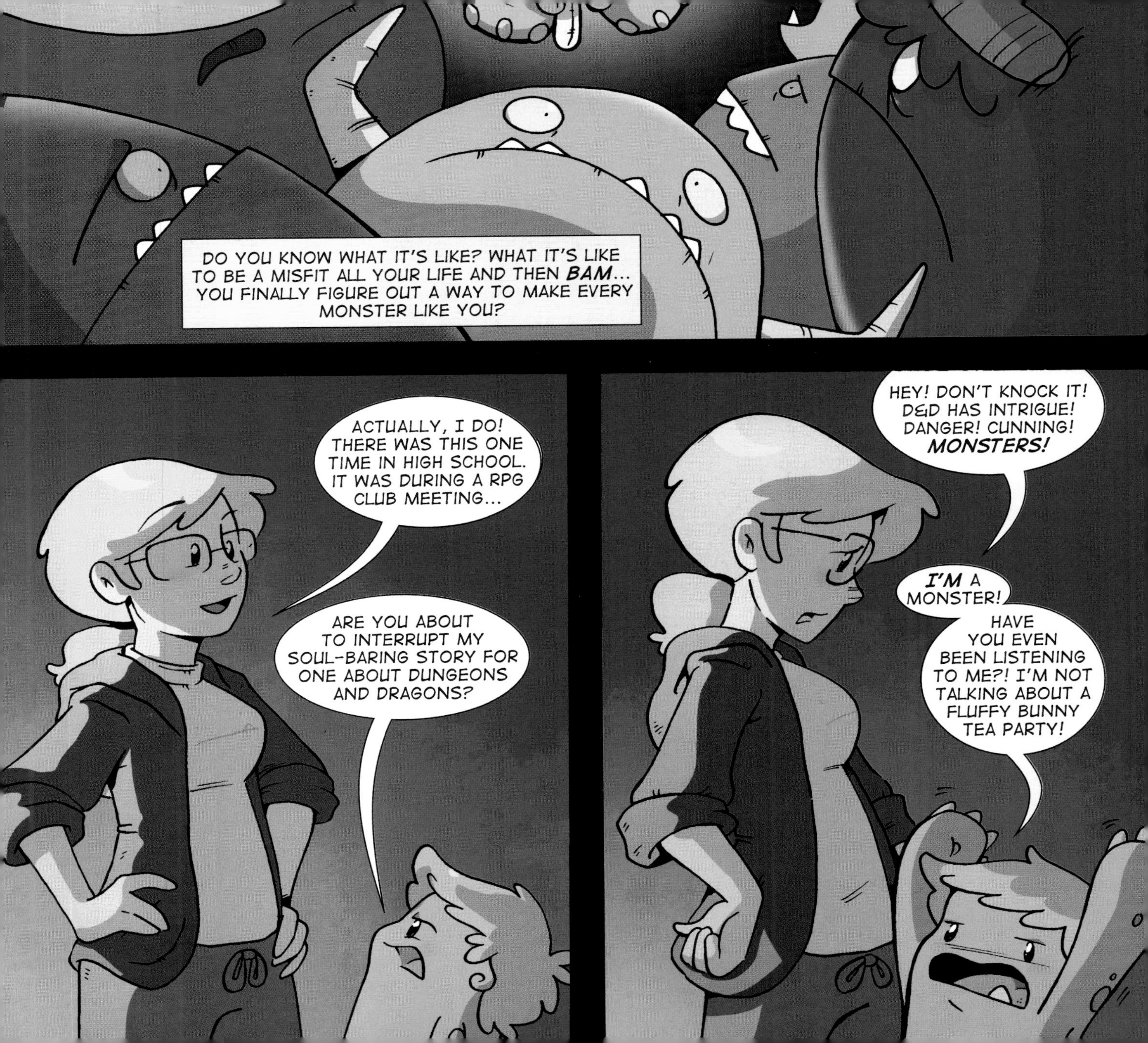
DO YOU KNOW WHAT IT'S LIKE? WHAT IT'S LIKE TO BE A MISFIT ALL YOUR LIFE AND THEN *BAM*... YOU FINALLY FIGURE OUT A WAY TO MAKE EVERY MONSTER LIKE YOU?
ACTUALLY, I DO! THERE WAS THIS ONE TIME IN HIGH SCHOOL. IT WAS DURING A RPG CLUB MEETING...
ARE YOU ABOUT TO INTERRUPT MY SOUL-BARING STORY FOR ONE ABOUT DUNGEONS AND DRAGONS?
HEY! DON'T KNOCK IT! D&D HAS INTRIGUE! DANGER! CUNNING! ***MONSTERS!***
*I'M* A MONSTER!
HAVE YOU EVEN BEEN LISTENING TO ME?! I'M NOT TALKING ABOUT A FLUFFY BUNNY TEA PARTY!

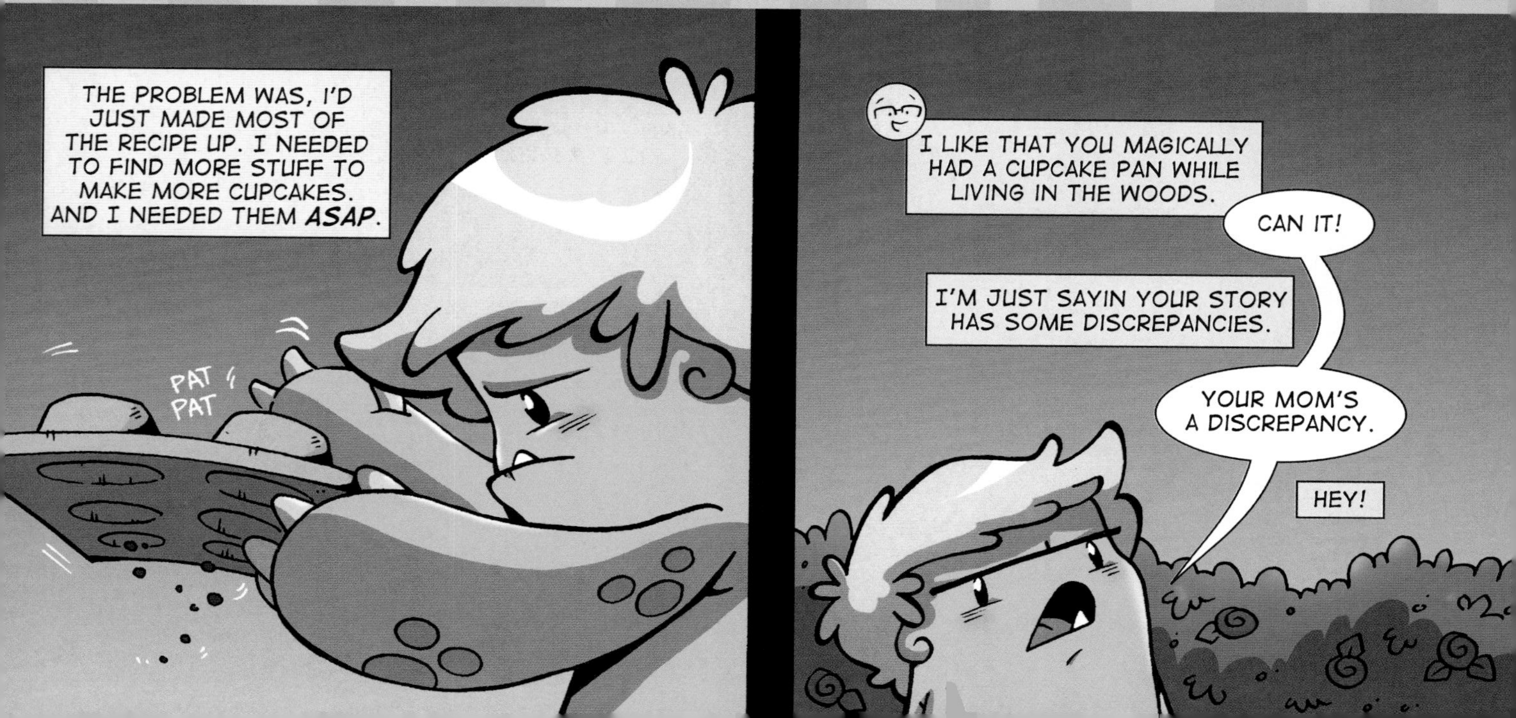
THE PROBLEM WAS, I'D JUST MADE MOST OF THE RECIPE UP. I NEEDED TO FIND MORE STUFF TO MAKE MORE CUPCAKES. AND I NEEDED THEM ***ASAP***.
PAT PAT
I LIKE THAT YOU MAGICALLY HAD A CUPCAKE PAN WHILE LIVING IN THE WOODS.
CAN IT!
I'M JUST SAYIN YOUR STORY HAS SOME DISCREPANCIES.
YOUR MOM'S A DISCREPANCY.
HEY!

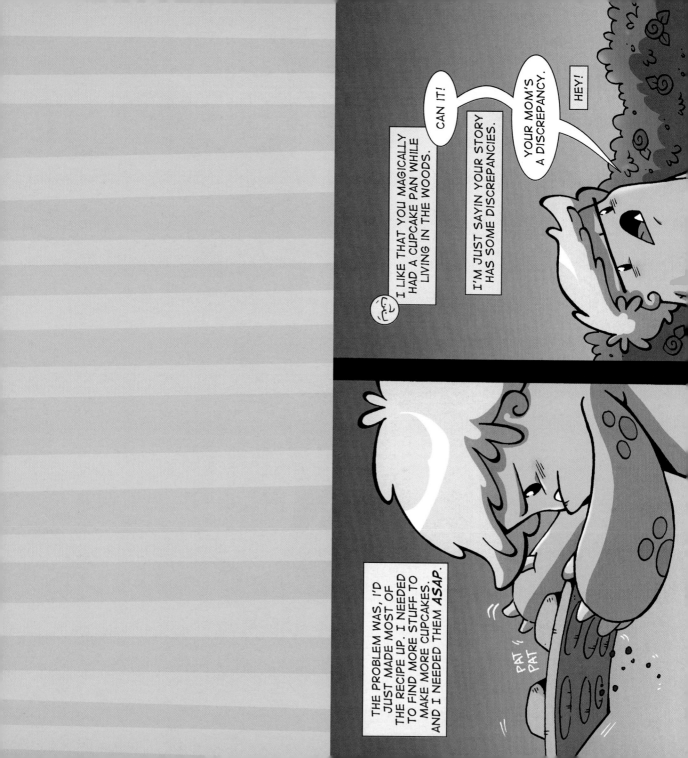

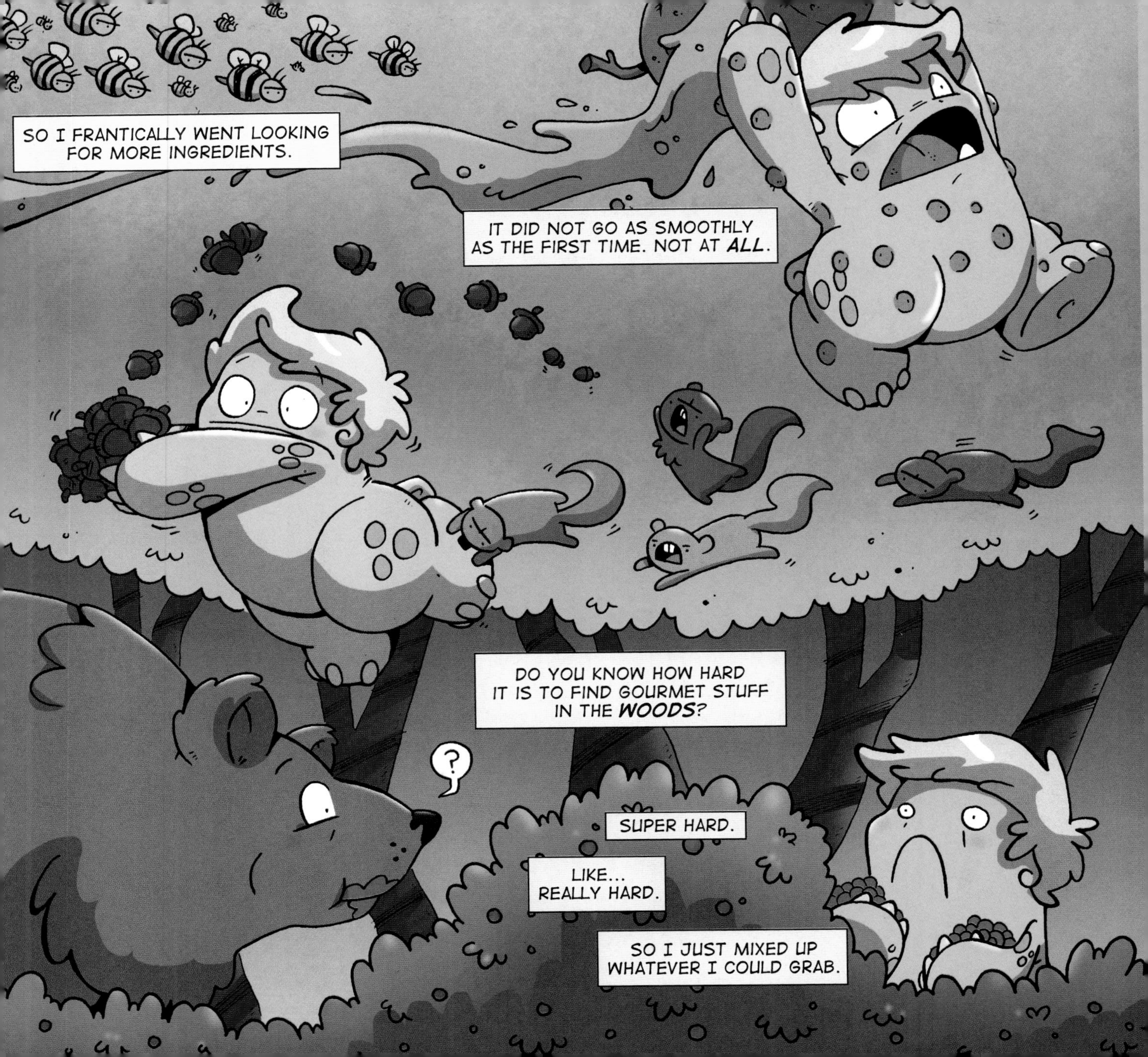
SO I FRANTICALLY WENT LOOKING FOR MORE INGREDIENTS.
IT DID NOT GO AS SMOOTHLY AS THE FIRST TIME. NOT AT *ALL*.
DO YOU KNOW HOW HARD IT IS TO FIND GOURMET STUFF IN THE *WOODS*?
?
SUPER HARD.
LIKE... REALLY HARD.
SO I JUST MIXED UP WHATEVER I COULD GRAB.

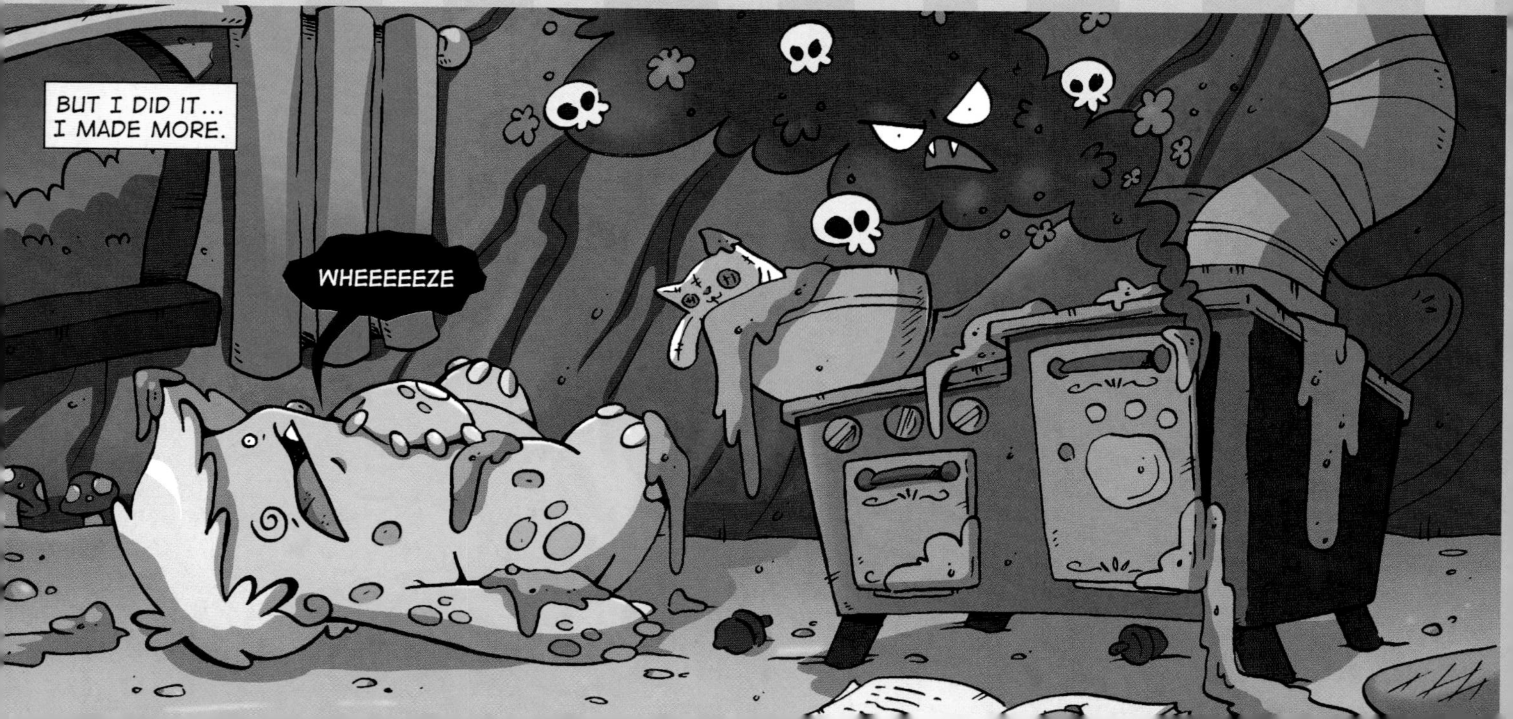
BUT I DID IT... I MADE MORE.
WHEEEEEEZE

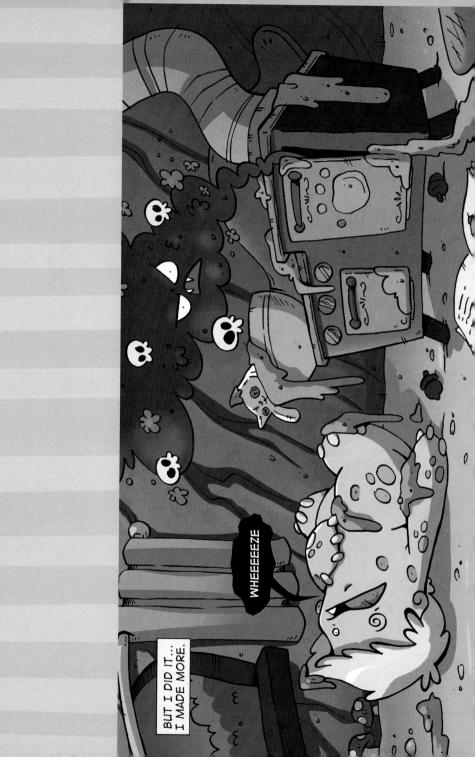

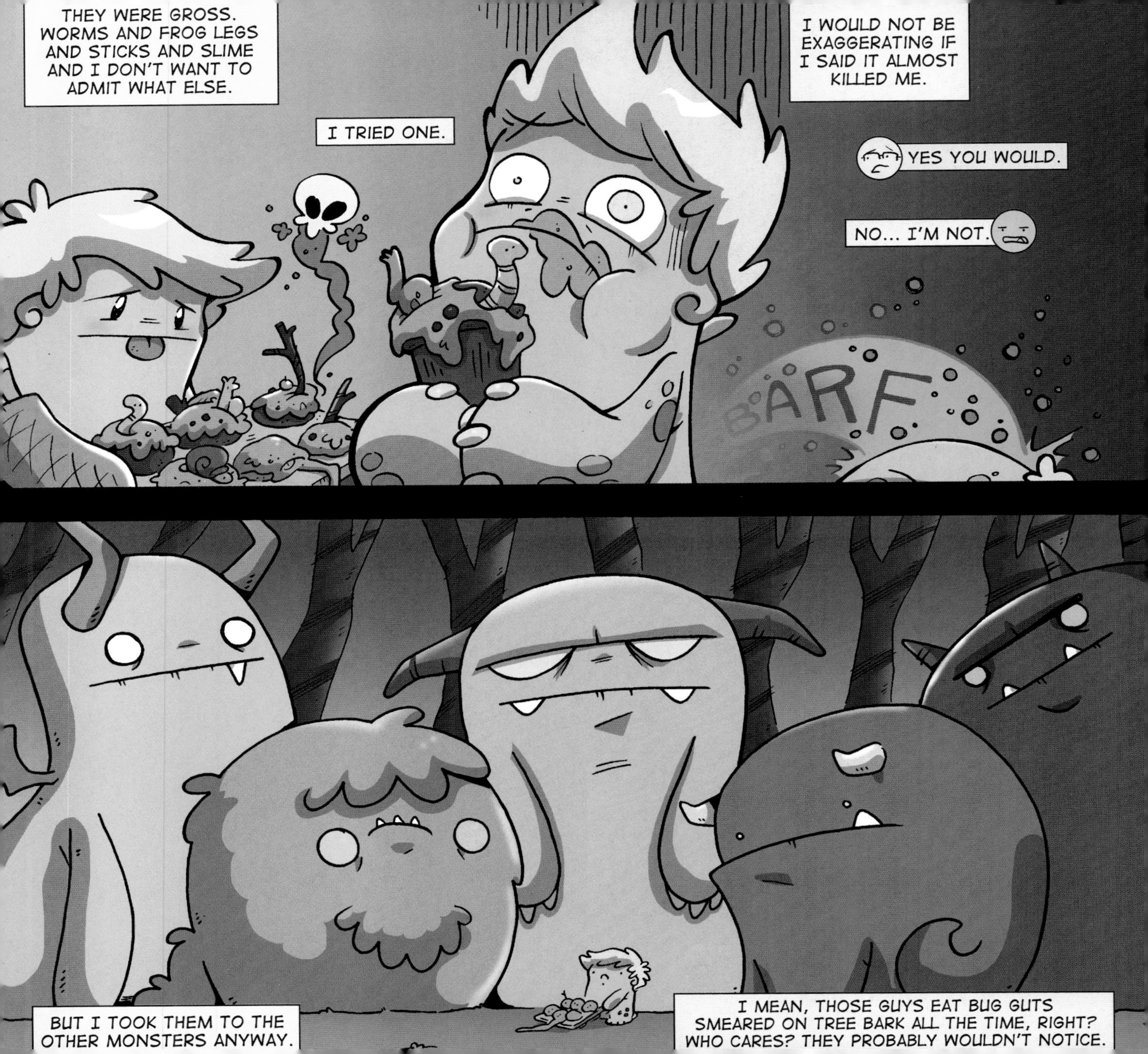
THEY WERE GROSS. WORMS AND FROG LEGS AND STICKS AND SLIME AND I DON'T WANT TO ADMIT WHAT ELSE.
I TRIED ONE.
I WOULD NOT BE EXAGGERATING IF I SAID IT ALMOST KILLED ME.
YES YOU WOULD.
NO... I'M NOT.
BARF
BUT I TOOK THEM TO THE OTHER MONSTERS ANYWAY.
I MEAN, THOSE GUYS EAT BUG GUTS SMEARED ON TREE BARK ALL THE TIME, RIGHT? WHO CARES? THEY PROBABLY WOULDN'T NOTICE.

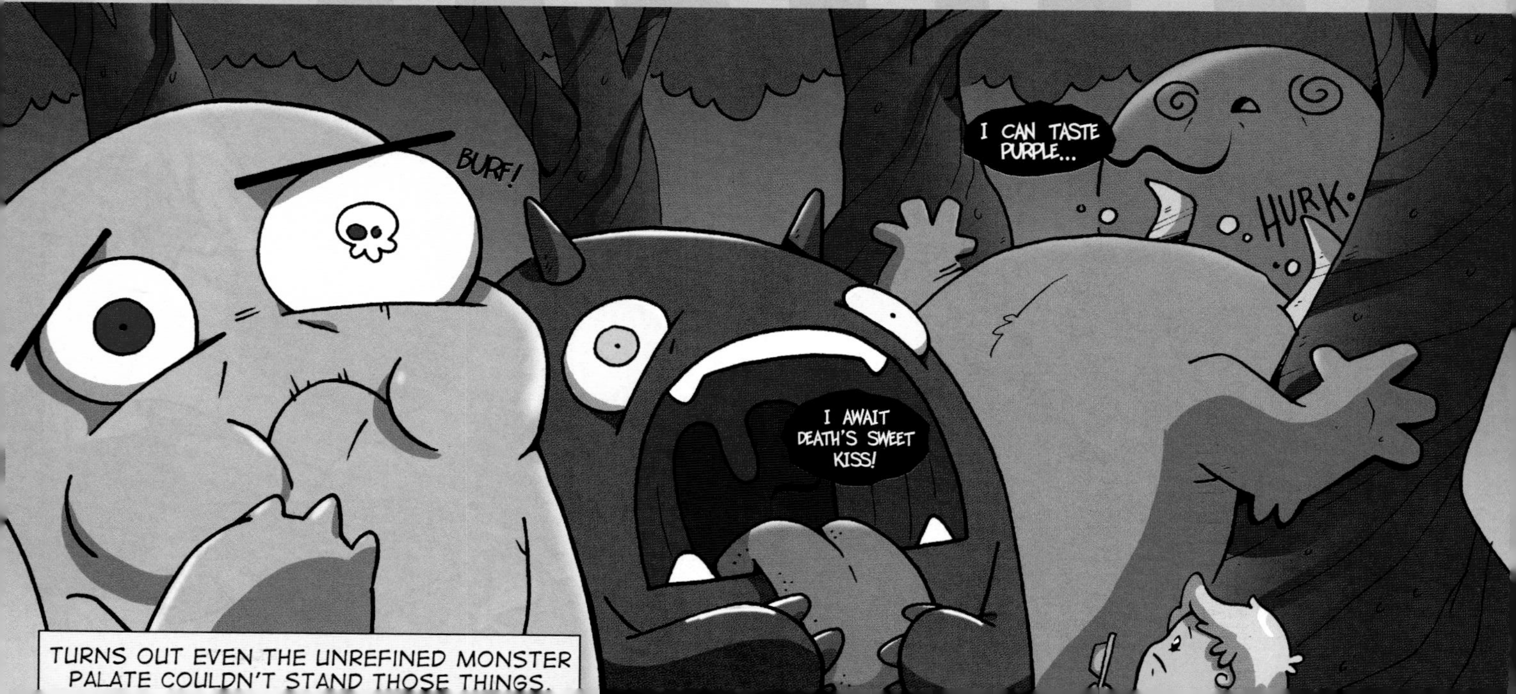
TURNS OUT EVEN THE UNREFINED MONSTER PALATE COULDN'T STAND THOSE THINGS.
BURF!
I AWAIT DEATH'S SWEET KISS!
I CAN TASTE PURPLE...
HURK.

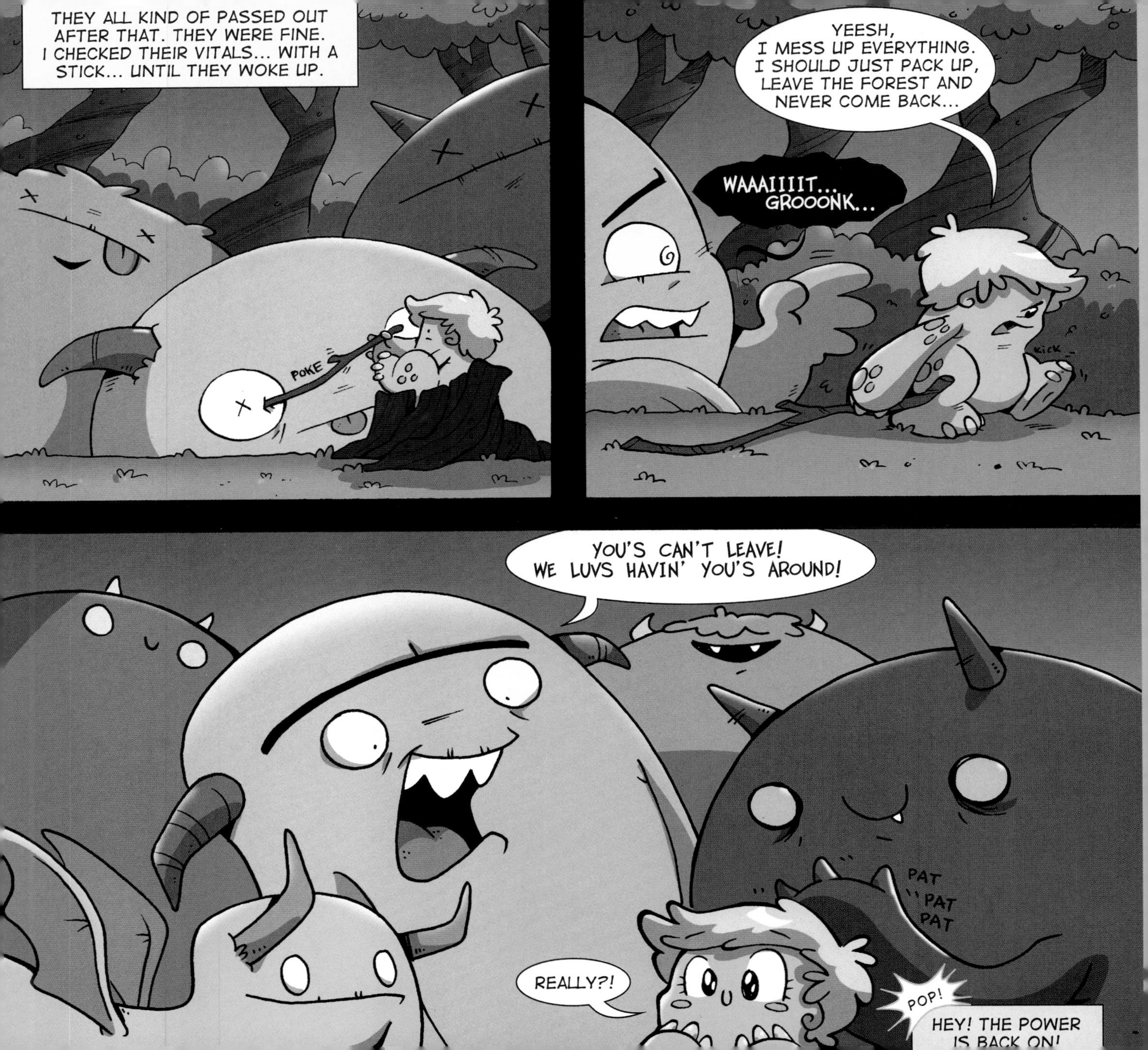
THEY ALL KIND OF PASSED OUT AFTER THAT. THEY WERE FINE. I CHECKED THEIR VITALS... WITH A STICK... UNTIL THEY WOKE UP.
POKE
YEESH, I MESS UP EVERYTHING. I SHOULD JUST PACK UP, LEAVE THE FOREST AND NEVER COME BACK...
WAAAIIIIT... GROOONK...
KICK
YOU'S CAN'T LEAVE! WE LUVS HAVIN' YOU'S AROUND!
PAT PAT PAT
REALLY?!
POP!
HEY! THE POWER IS BACK ON!

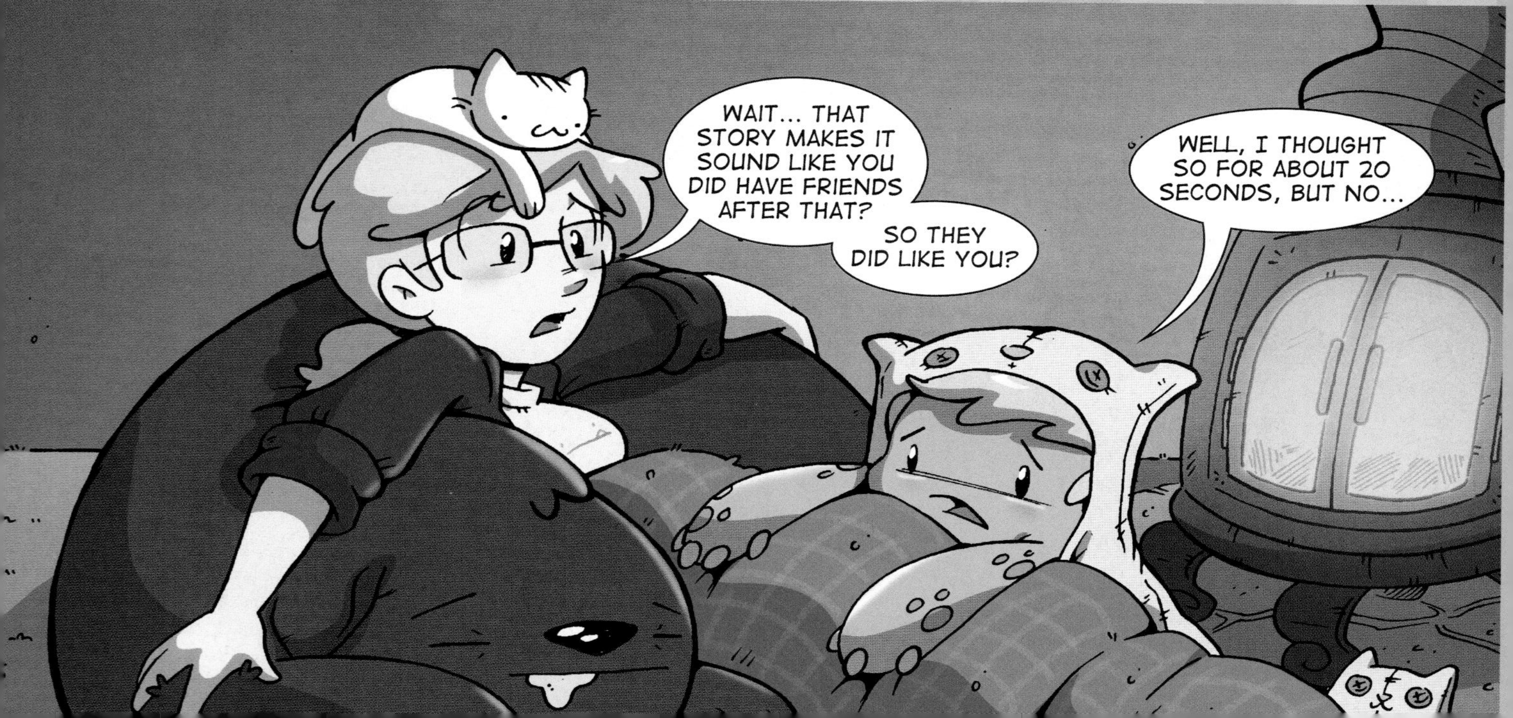
WAIT... THAT STORY MAKES IT SOUND LIKE YOU DID HAVE FRIENDS AFTER THAT?
SO THEY DID LIKE YOU?
WELL, I THOUGHT SO FOR ABOUT 20 SECONDS, BUT NO...

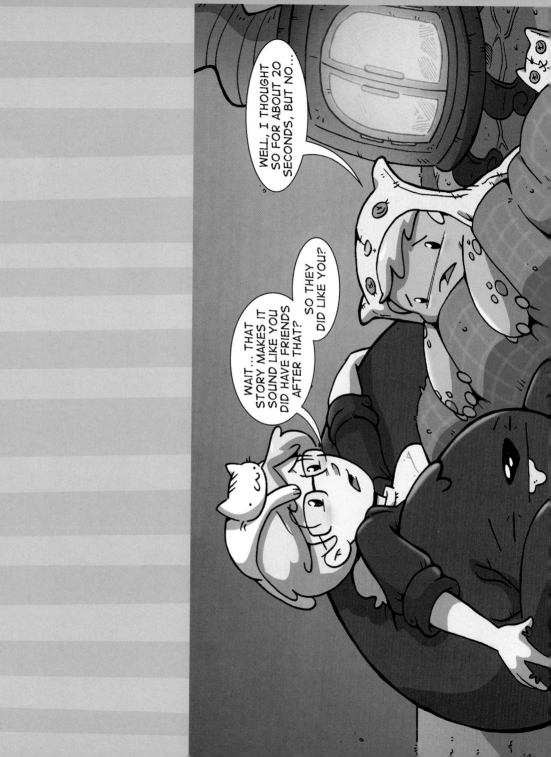

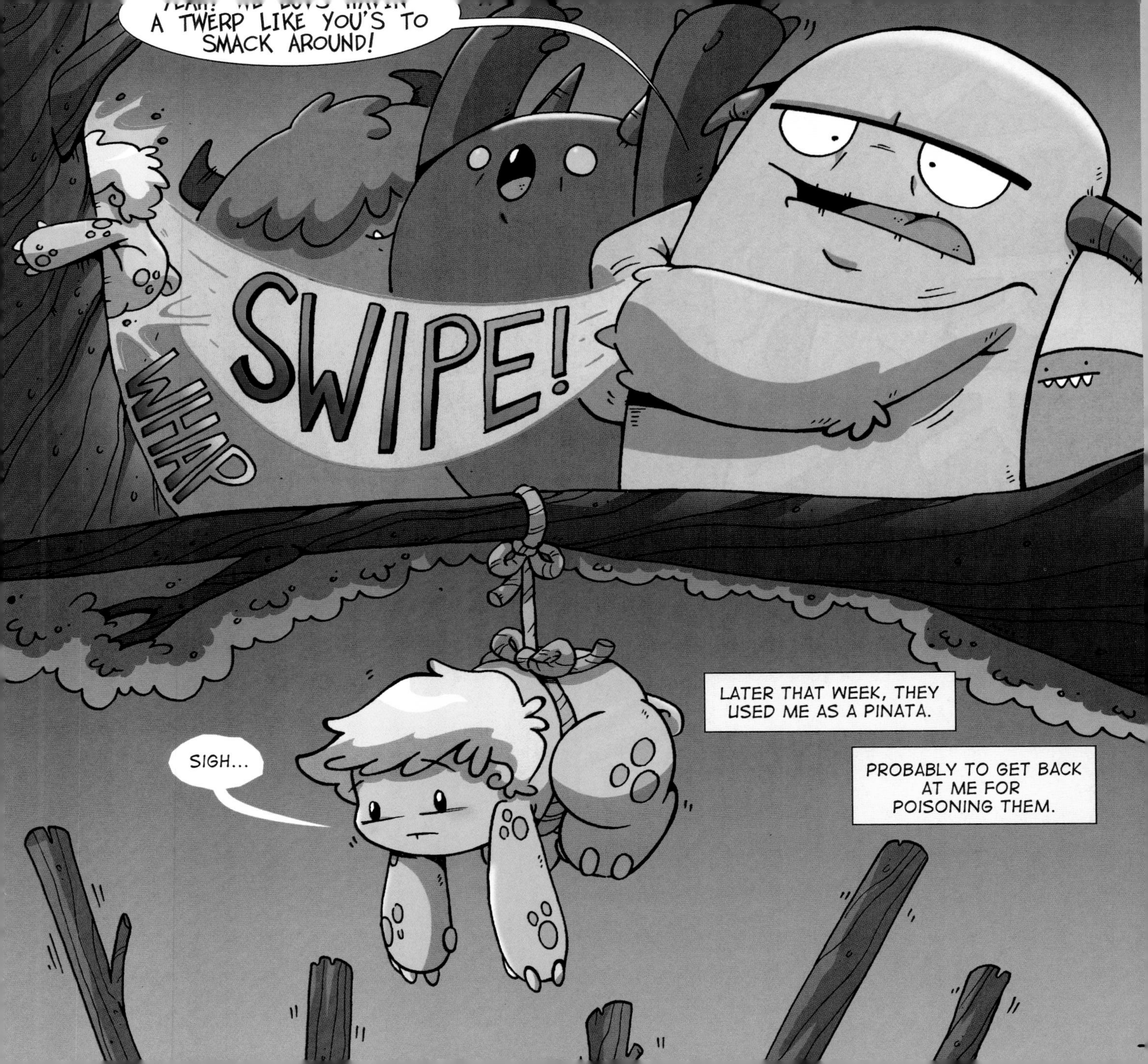
A TWERP LIKE YOU'S TO SMACK AROUND!
SWIPE!
WHAP
LATER THAT WEEK, THEY USED ME AS A PINATA.
PROBABLY TO GET BACK AT ME FOR POISONING THEM.
SIGH...

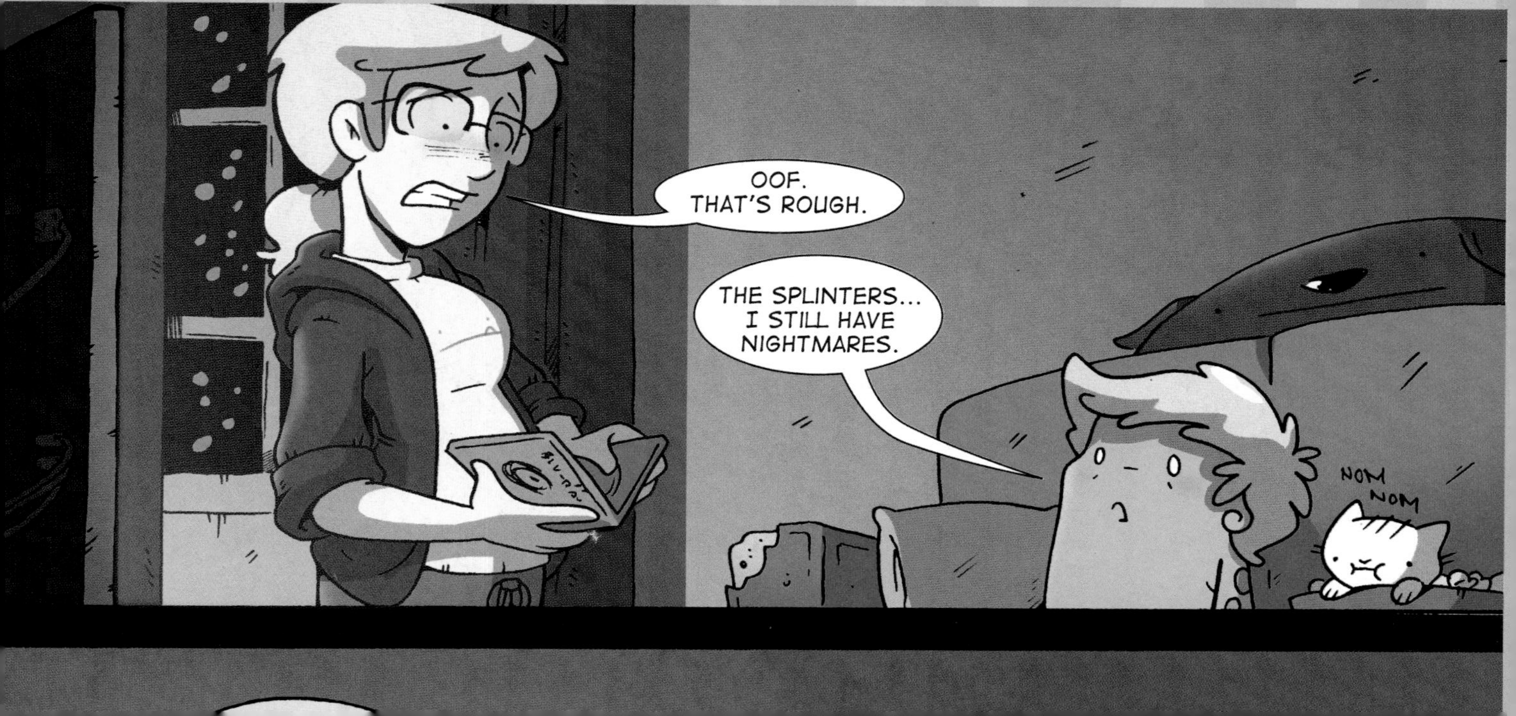
OOF.
THAT'S ROUGH.
THE SPLINTERS... I STILL HAVE NIGHTMARES.
NOM NOM

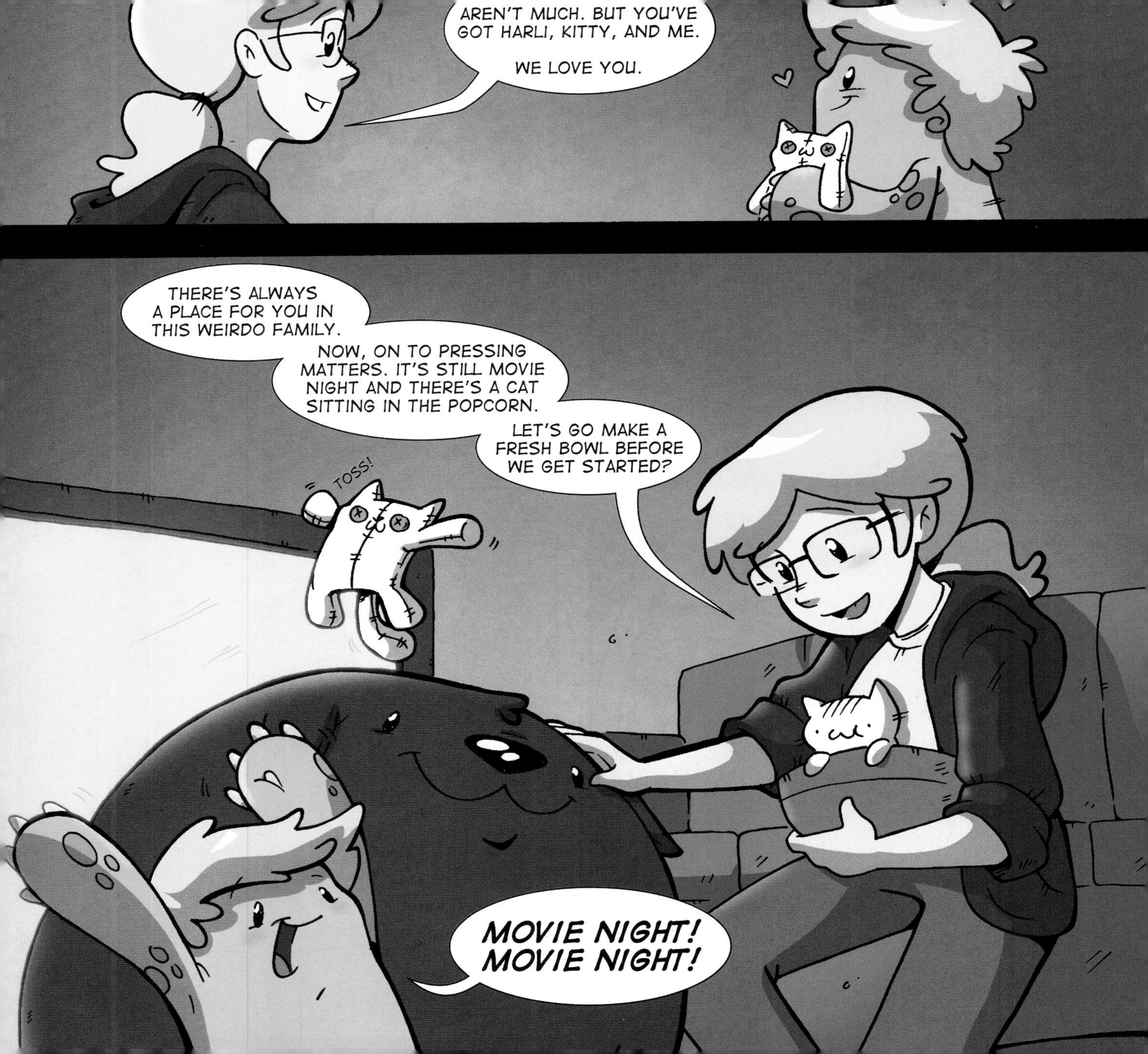
AREN'T MUCH. BUT YOU'VE GOT HARLI, KITTY, AND ME.
WE LOVE YOU.
THERE'S ALWAYS A PLACE FOR YOU IN THIS WEIRDO FAMILY.
NOW, ON TO PRESSING MATTERS. IT'S STILL MOVIE NIGHT AND THERE'S A CAT SITTING IN THE POPCORN.
LET'S GO MAKE A FRESH BOWL BEFORE WE GET STARTED?
TOSS!
MOVIE NIGHT! MOVIE NIGHT!